AF529138

# I named my sister Silence

Translated by
Hansda Sowvendra Shekhar

Manoj Rupda

# I named my sister Silence

eka

eka

First published in Hindi as *Kaale Adhyaay* in 2015 by Bharatiya Jnanpith

Published in English as *I Named My Sister Silence* in 2023 by Eka, an imprint of Westland Books, a division of Nasadiya Technologies Private Limited

No. 269/2B, First Floor, 'Irai Arul', Vimalraj Street, Nethaji Nagar, Alapakkam Main Road, Maduravoyal, Chennai 600095

Westland, the Westland logo, Eka and the Eka logo are the trademarks of Nasadiya Technologies Private Limited, or its affiliates.

Original Copyright © Manoj Rupda, 2015
Translation Copyright © Hansda Sowvendra Shekhar, 2023

Manoj Rupda asserts the moral right to be identified as the author of this work.

ISBN: 9789357765770

10 9 8 7 6 5 4 3 2 1

This is a work of fiction. Names, characters, organisations, places, events and incidents are either products of the author's imagination or used fictitiously.

All rights reserved

Typeset by Jojy Philip, New Delhi 110 015

Printed at Parksons Graphics Pvt. Ltd

No part of this book may be reproduced, or stored in a retrieval system, or transmitted in any form or by any means, electronic, mechanical, photocopying, recording, or otherwise, without express written permission of the publisher.

# Contents

# Prologue

It hurts differently to watch something immense and majestic fall lifelessly to its knees and be taken apart by powers beyond its control.

Like a ship being dismantled by cutting machines and cranes.

Like an elephant being eaten alive by wild dogs.

Like a forest being mined and ravaged by corporates.

It hurts much the same way to be left alone.

By a mentor.

By a co-traveller.

By one's own sister.

Part 1

# The Forest

## CHAPTER 1

# Graveyard

The ship-breaking yard at Alang in Gujarat, on the Gulf of Khambat, is supposed to be the largest in the world. It is where ships go to die. Or, to be precise, it is where ships are taken to be slaughtered. Our ship was called Jaldoot—The Water Messenger—and it too had been brought to this graveyard of ships. As I stood in the yard looking at my ship, I wondered if it was my destiny to witness the death of everything that was huge, everything that had enamoured me with its sheer size, everything that I held dear.

In my backpack, I had the diary that belonged to Captain Alok Datt. I would like to say that the diary still belongs to Captain Datt. But I can't. Captain Datt left. Disappeared. I don't know if he will even return to claim his diary in which there are words about nature and life; words as bitter as Captain Datt himself had been. The diary had been torn, its pages ripped out, and I found it in the debris inside Captain Datt's cabin.

I looked at the entire length of the ship. I had looked at it the same way when I joined as the Third Engineer on this ship about two years ago. But, now, it wasn't I alone who was looking at the ship. The ship was looking back at me, perhaps making it known that it was dying. I was only at the end of my job; the ship was at the end of its life.

I have no idea why I am fond of large things. And I have no idea why I have always been destined to witness the disintegration of those large things. In my childhood, I had seen an elephant die. After that, I saw my community disintegrate. Now, I would watch the breaking down of the ship where I worked, a ship that did not deserve to die. At least, not now; not so soon. But then, that elephant too did not deserve to die, nor did our community, nor did our forest. Do we all get what we deserve? Is it that simple?

I am surrounded by memories but I try to remain untouched, unmoved. In my memories, there is, on the one hand, the ship which is about to be killed in the breaking yard, and on the other hand, there is a burning forest and my community that has already been killed. One after the other, all those memories come tumbling down in my mind. I will them to return to the place they came from.

But no. How does one turn memories around?

And how can I push away the memories of that elephant?

CHAPTER 2

# Elephant

I saw an elephant once. I was ten years old and a student of class five at the time. I lived in the village of Basamura in Bastar. I had never seen an animal as huge as an elephant before. I was on my way to school, with my school bag filled with books and a slate on my back. The elephant stood in the middle of the village. There were children, women and some elderly people surrounding it.

The older people placed 25 paise and 50 paise coins in the finger of the elephant's trunk, bowed before it and moved away. The elephant raised its trunk and handed the coins to the mahout sitting on its back. Some women had brought *gud laddoo,* made of grains and jaggery; other women had brought *thethri* and *khurmi,* snacks made of wheat flour and jaggery. They placed the sweets and snacks in the crook of the elephant's trunk. Some women also put cucumbers and carrots in it. Instead of handing those over to the mahout, the elephant gobbled them up.

When no one was left to offer anything else to the elephant, the mahout struck the elephant's ears with both his big toes and the elephant began to walk away. I hated to see it walking away. So many people were seeing the elephant moving away, but there was a difference in the way they saw it and the way I did. They were all bidding a joyous farewell to the elephant, whereas I had been totally mesmerised by the giant creature. After some time, the women and the elderly people walked back towards their homes and the children walked towards the school, but I began to walk after the elephant and followed it outside the village.

I walked after the elephant for a long time. I didn't know what it was that was pulling me towards the elephant. Even after I had crossed the village limits, I wasn't aware of how far I had walked. I just kept trailing after the elephant.

I had left the village behind and entered the forest, forgetting everything and everyone—my village, my house, my father, my mother, my sister, my school, my teacher, all my friends. None of them figured in my mind anymore. Even after walking for more than an hour, I had neither any worry nor any fear. I could see only the elephant before me and the man atop it who was blowing out clouds of smoke from a beedi and rocking from side to side as the elephant walked.

The path we were on was covered with dried leaves. Not only the path, the entire forest floor was covered with dried leaves. For a long way ahead, only dried leaves could be seen. The sound of my feet walking over those dried leaves was muffled by the sound of the elephant's feet crushing them.

The mahout could not hear that there was someone walking behind them.

I lagged behind as I tried to hear the sound of my footsteps. By the time I looked up, the elephant had moved ahead. Frightened, I ran after it, and as I did so, the sound of the dried leaves being crushed under my feet turned more furious than when the elephant had plodded over them.

The sound of my running made the elephant stop. The mahout blew a puff of smoke and turned around. I stopped running and the mahout's eyes met mine. He looked at me for some time and then, lifting his right leg, turned around completely towards me.

'Where did you come from?' He looked stunned.

'From Basamura,' I said, panting a little.

'Which village?'

'Basamura.'

'Basamura? You've come from Basamura?'

'Yes.'

'You're alone?'

I nodded my head in the affirmative.

'Why did you come so far into the jungle?'

'To see the elephant.'

The mahout turned speechless for a moment.

'You came so far from your village just to see the elephant?'

I said nothing. The man's nervous voice had scared me. He looked very worried. He turned back towards the elephant's head and gently patted its shoulder. The elephant stooped and sat down unwillingly.

Then the mahout turned towards me and gestured at me to go to him. I walked slowly towards him. As I reached close to the elephant, it turned its trunk towards me. Scared, I moved a few steps back. But then the elephant blinked its eye at me and shook its ears, and I wasn't scared anymore.

The mahout extended his right hand towards me and I grabbed it. He pulled me up on the elephant. My feet got caught in the dirty rags spread on the elephant's back and my school bag turned upside down. The mahout kept holding me till I had settled comfortably on the elephant's back. Then he put his arm around my body and tapped the elephant's ears with his stick. The elephant stamped one foot on the ground and then another, and as it swayed from side to side, I screamed in fear.

It was the first time I had climbed atop a moving object. When the elephant started walking gently, the mahout removed his hand from around my body. Some time later, I too got accustomed to riding an elephant. My fear vanished.

'You shouldn't have come so far into the forest,' the mahout told me. 'You are very young. There are wild dogs, bears and buffaloes in this forest. They are very dangerous.'

He started telling me scary stories about forests from here and there. My attention was not on his stories but on the beautiful scenery of the forest. A little ahead, there was a tree laden with bright red flowers. It was a pleasant sight to behold—a tree covered with bright, red flowers in the middle of an arid, lonely forest. There were colourful birds chirping on its branches. Upon spotting the elephant, their chirping became louder. The parrots were the loudest, as if they were teasing the elephant. When the elephant raised its trunk, the birds flew away from the tree, but after flying in a circle, they returned to the tree and hid themselves among its flowers.

I saw several such trees laden with red flowers as we moved deeper into the forest. The entire path was lined with these trees and there were so many flowers on the ground that as far as I could see, the forest floor was covered in red.

After some time, we left the flower-laden trees behind and were again surrounded by thorny bushes and dried leaves. Now I could hear only the rustling of the dried leaves beneath the feet of the elephant.

'There is a village ahead,' the mahout said to me. 'I will drop you there. There must be someone there who would know you. They'll take you back to your village.'

I nodded my head.

But the mahout's guess was wrong. The forest ahead was denser and there was no sign of any village. All we could see were dried bushes around us and dried leaves below. The layer of dried leaves on the ground was so dense that the elephant's feet dug through the leaves as it walked. After a while, it was hard to tell which way we were headed. The parallel rows of trees by the path were gone. Instead, we found ourselves stuck in a space made narrow by bushes and leaves that seemed to have grown all together and at the same time. There must have been a track, but it had been made invisible by all the dried leaves fallen on the ground.

The mahout pulled the chain tied around the elephant's neck with both his hands and it stopped. I turned around and saw worry and annoyance lining the mahout's face. He was looking around, trying to figure something out. There was total silence for some time. And then, the bushes to our right began stirring and we heard a crackling sound. Although we could not see what was happening inside the bushes, the mahout sensed what that movement and sound could be. He immediately tugged at the chain tied around the elephant's neck and rapped it on both its ears with his stick. The elephant broke into a run.

After some time, we reached a clearing in the forest. There were no bushes there and the entire place was covered with tall trees. The mahout stopped the elephant near a banyan tree. He wiped the sweat from his brow with a gamchha and stood on the elephant's back. Standing akimbo, he looked in all directions but couldn't determine which way to go. After standing for several moments in that position, he tied the gamchha around his waist and climbed on to a branch hanging close to the elephant's head. He balanced himself on all fours on the branch and, holding it tightly, began climbing upwards. He reached that part of the tree where the stronger branches ended and the softer, more supple branches began. He moved those softer branches apart and looked all around to find a path.

I kept looking at the mahout. He appeared even more worried than before. It seemed as if he was trying to come to a decision, but, finally, he just shook his head in resignation and began muttering something. He untied the gamchha from his waist, wiped his face again with it, wrapped it around his neck, and returned to the elephant's back.

'What were you looking at from the tree?' I asked him when he had settled himself on the elephant's back.

'Shut up, you dunce!' He snapped at me all of a sudden. 'I'm lost because of you.'

I felt stung by this unexpected outburst. Tears welled up in my eyes, but the man showed no mercy.

After some time, he took the hatchet tucked inside a rope tied around the elephant's body and threw it on the ground. Then he loosened the rope and, holding its open end, climbed down from the elephant's body. Then he tied the chain wound around the elephant's neck to the trunk of the banyan tree.

The mahout did not look at me even once. I couldn't gauge what he was thinking or what he intended to do. He checked the knot of the elephant's tether, picked up the hatchet and walked away into the bushes. When he did not return for a long time, I looked around at the desolation in which he had left me alone.

The sun's rays started turning pale. The day was coming to a close. A cool breeze started blowing, shaking the leaves in the trees and blowing away the ones that were scattered on the forest floor. When the breeze stopped, I saw the sun, a big red ball, descending in the west into the bushes.

I could feel only two beings breathing in that expansive quiet. The elephant and I. I was shivering and the elephant seemed anxious. I had never seen an animal as huge as the elephant. I had heard that no other animal on earth was as big and strong as the elephant. I used to imagine how big an elephant must be, but this elephant was bigger than I had imagined.

Dusk came in some time. The clamouring of birds quietened. Darkness fell. Can you imagine the kind of thoughts that crossed the mind of a ten-year-old boy caught in a situation like that? At night, in a forest, sitting atop an elephant chained to a tree.

Surrounded by darkness and quiet inside the forest, tired and hungry, that boy fell asleep sitting atop the elephant. The tiredness from the seven-hour walk and the cool breeze of the forest lulled him to sleep.

The boy slept for a long time. Sounds of crawling, rustling and footsteps came from the forest. These were the footsteps of hunger that were slowly making their way to the elephant. Slowly, very slowly, a circle was being created around the elephant. The circle shone with several bright, red eyes. Those eyes first stared at each other, then growled, and then disappeared into the darkness—only to appear again.

The elephant was alerted by the growling. It saw the red eyes moving closer. The elephant used its trunk like a weapon and started swinging it towards those red eyes.

Those eyes belonged to wild dogs whose unity and co-ordination with one another was quite something. The elephant wasn't a wild one, it had been tamed, and was used to going from one place to another begging food and money from humans. What did it know about surviving in the wild? It had never seen wild dogs hunting in a pack. It was familiar only with dogs in villages, dogs that lived with humans, dogs which only barked on spotting an elephant and kept on barking till the elephant had left the village.

The wild dogs were not barking. There was a secret communication taking place among them. As soon as the elephant started swinging its trunk, the wild dogs separated into two groups and, shaking their bushy tails in front of the elephant, disappeared. However hard it tried, the elephant could not see where those wild dogs went as its neck was tied to the banyan tree with an iron chain.

When the next few moments passed uneventfully, the elephant loosened its body and its eyes began to droop.

But then—the elephant trumpeted loudly all of a sudden and, with a furious force, began shaking both its hind legs. The boy, wide awake, could not understand what was happening, but he had enough presence of mind to hold on tightly to the chain tied around the elephant's neck. Having secured himself, the boy looked down at the ground and his breathing nearly stopped. Nearly twenty wild dogs clung to both the hind legs of the elephant and were eating it. Not only that, more wild dogs were coming closer to join the previous pack.

The oncoming wild dogs were bigger and looked more ferocious than the ones clinging to the elephant's legs. They too circled the elephant, silently communicating among themselves, and jumped upon the previous pack to claim their share of the elephant's body. The forest reverberated with the shrieks of the elephant and the attacking dogs the elephant had trampled under its feet. The elephant began shaking its entire body with such force that it seemed as if the branches of the banyan tree would break and fall off.

Some time later, though, the elephant turned silent. It lowered its trunk and stopped trying to free its legs from the grip of the wild dogs.

After some time, it began lowering its hind legs, slowly, like a ship sinking in a sea after being wrecked in an accident.

The boy grew alert. He stood up while still holding on to the chain tied around the elephant's neck. He steadied himself and then grabbed the trunk of the banyan tree. He clung to the tree with his arms and, slowly, lifted his feet off the elephant's body. Then, crawling like a quadruped, the boy climbed up the tree.

The elephant was down. The two packs of wild dogs too had stopped fighting with one another. A silent arrangement had been made between them. The larger ones began tearing into the thick hide of the elephant while the smaller ones tore the flesh after the hide had been taken off. When the dogs reached the abdomen of the elephant, they were perhaps assured that they wouldn't need to hunt for the next three days at least, so they too slowed down their biting and tearing.

Now that they did not have to worry about food, the dogs turned quiet. The elephant too was at peace, for it had given itself up completely to the dogs, allowing them to devour its body.

Sitting high up on a banyan tree on a full-moon night, that ten-year-old boy witnessed the destruction of the largest animal he had ever seen in his life. He stared at the expressionless eye of the elephant gleaming in the moonlight. Sometimes the elephant blinked its eye; sometimes it fixed it up on the sky, on the moon and the stars. When a particular bite was too painful, the elephant raised its head and shook its neck a bit, and then it again lowered its head and resumed staring at the sky.

A cool breeze began blowing. The leaves of the banyan tree began rustling. Birds chirped. The boy did not realise when he dropped upon the thick branch and fell asleep once again.

Day broke and the forest was resonant with the chirping of birds. The boy kept sleeping. He woke up only when the redness of the sun had turned white and a stream of sun rays fell directly on his face.

The first thing the boy saw upon waking up was the head of the elephant. Its neck had turned to one side. Its eye was open and frozen, and two crows were taking turns with their beaks. The lower part of the elephant's body had been claimed by kites, vultures and more crows. Its belly was torn open and two hyenas had sunk into it, digging and eating. After some digging, the hyenas left, dragging huge chunks of meat with them. Apart from the larger scavengers, there were also smaller ones, like ants of various kinds. The elephant had voluntarily provided food for a good part of the forest.

Such an event could either scar a person or make them fearless for life. Something similar happened with that boy too. The death of the elephant ended all innocence and childish fears. The change was obvious. The boy climbed down from the tree and, just like that, started walking on a track.

That boy was, of course, me, but I cannot say what kind of thoughts were playing in the mind of that boy at the time. Either he wasn't thinking at all or he had developed a separate consciousness of his own. The way a pair of twins develop within the same womb, two separate streams of thought were working in my mind.

At the time of choosing that track, the boy didn't know how long and arduous it would be. He found another corpse along the track, as mangled as the carcass of the elephant. All the bones in that corpse had been broken and sucked dry. Beside it lay a hatchet, a red gamchha and an amulet tied with a black thread. The boy stared at the corpse for some time, then he picked up the hatchet and walked away.

It is difficult to imagine the thoughts that came to the boy's mind upon seeing the bodies of the elephant and the mahout. The thing is: the boy had changed by the time he walked out of the forest. He was a human only in his body, his mind had turned as devoid of thought as that of an animal.

When I grew up, I came to know that there were two humans growing within me: one, who was fascinated by everything big; and the Other, who accepted every destruction as easily and without any thought as an animal. And that the Other had come with me from the forest.

## CHAPTER 3

# Sister

Unable to find my way out, I wandered in the forest for two days. My entire family was stunned when I finally reached home. Some forest ranger had handed them my school bag just the previous day, and they were waiting for my dead body to arrive.

My father received me with a tight slap on my face. I fell far away from him, but I stood up the next moment. I neither looked at him nor touched my face where he had slapped me. With a voice steeped in sadness and emotions, he started scolding me. Buba was quite brash and sported an impressive moustache, so it was quite strange to see him talking in that emotion-filled voice.

My mother leapt on me like an untamed animal and cried loudly. However, there wasn't a tear in her eyes, and her crying and screaming did not touch me at all. In fact, instead of being touched, I was repulsed. My uncle—my father's younger brother—and his wife, and other men and women from the neighbourhood circled me. Their collective response to my disappearance and unexpected return was so fake that I felt I would have been better off dead.

I looked at the crowd and couldn't see any hint of sympathy; yet, they were displaying concern as humans are wont to. I wasn't there. Everyone was talking to me, they were touching me. Yet, I wasn't there. I was in the forest, staring at the eye of the elephant gleaming in the moonlight. The last time the elephant looked at me before it died.

In reality, I wasn't in the forest. I was in my village, among humans, with my family. Yet, I don't know why, despite being subjected to all those overt expressions of human concern, the only thing on my mind was that last time when the elephant had looked at me. I am yet to understand why even now, whenever anything momentous happens to me, I am reminded of that elephant and its eyes staring at the sky in that moonlit night. How grave the look in its eyes was. It made all the notions I had held about the world until then seem inconsequential.

I did not talk to anyone that day. My silence hurt Yaya very much. She shook me repeatedly so that I would say something. But no, I spoke not one word. Had I shed a tear, perhaps my mother would have been assured that I was all right. But I gave no response of any kind. Finally, she started crying, calling aloud the name of Goddess Danteshwari, the presiding deity of Dantewada.

My uncle came then and dragged Yaya away from me.

'Move, sister-in-law! Let *me* deal with this boy!' he declared in anger.

He grabbed my arm and said to me, 'What? Don't you feel any pity for your mother? Look how she is crying! Tearing her throat apart. Why are you staring like a duffer? Go to your mother and stop her crying.'

He pushed me towards Yaya. But instead of going towards her, I moved away. Something had really happened to me that day, for I kept staring at my mother, my eyes unblinking. My uncle came and gave me a slap. But, just as when my father slapped me, I neither touched my face nor stirred from where I stood. That angered my uncle even more. He shouted, 'Wait! You just wait! I'll drive this spirit out of you. You aren't one to listen to reason. A few whips on your buttocks—only that will make you listen.'

Saying that, he actually brought the whip that was used to whip bullocks from his bullock cart. No one stopped him. On the contrary, the crowd made way for him to do his work efficiently.

But then, Irma Kako, my elder sister, blocked my uncle's path. She stopped him.

Buba, my father, had two wives. Kako, my elder sister, who was seven years older than me, was the child of the elder wife who was dead. I was the child of my father's second wife, my Yaya.

My sister grabbed my arm, pushed the crowd away, and took me inside the house. She took me into the room that I shared with her and bolted the door from the inside. My uncle was shouting at her from outside the house. Yaya too joined him and shouted the dirtiest of expletives at my sister. It was clear that my mother had no love for her stepdaughter. She accused her of spoiling me. But my sister went about doing what she had to do without paying any attention to what others said.

My sister's room had a door that opened into our garden at the rear of the house. She opened the door and tucked the end of her sari into her waist. She came to me and, without saying a word to me, unbuttoned my shirt and took it off. Then she took off my shorts. She then walked me to the well in the garden and made me sit on the large stone on which we washed clothes and utensils. She pulled a bucket of water from the well and poured all the water on my body. Then she pulled out another bucket of water and kept it aside. Then she took a soap and rubbed it between her palms, working up a nice amount of sud. She rubbed those suds on my face and cleaned it. I closed my eyes. After cleaning my face, she rubbed soap on my head and all over my body. Then she poured the second bucket of water over me. I opened my eyes and saw her going about her work silently. I wanted to understand what made her give me such a thorough bath. Had she become aware of the Other who had come with me from the forest? Was she determined to wash off the Other from my body?

My sister held my hand and brought me into her room. She dried my body with a gamchha and put fresh clothes on me. She put coconut oil on my head and combed my hair. Then holding both my hands tightly with her left hand, she took the box of kajal from a niche in the wall with her right hand.

She held my hands tightly because I never allowed her to put kajal in my eyes. I would scream and try my best to wriggle out of her grip whenever she tried. She, on her part, would grab me even more firmly and would not let me escape till she had put the kajal. Often, in that tussle between us, the kajal would spread on my face. She would wipe it off and, instead of lining my eyes with it, put a large dot on the left side of my forehead. I hated that dot more than having the kajal in my eyes. That day, though, I did not protest. I peacefully let my sister put kajal in my eyes.

When I was ready, she probably noticed that some strands of my hair were standing on end, so she combed it once again. Then she took a good look at my face. On her face, I saw worry. Unlike the loud and even physical expressions of worry from the others, my sister's worry was a silent one. She was trying to understand, wordlessly, what had happened to me. She kept looking at me for some time, then opened the door of her room.

Outside, Yaya had spread garbage all over the kitchen floor. My mother often spread garbage here and there to trouble my sister. She never missed an opportunity to trouble my sister. I never understood the reason for my mother's hatred, but I hated her for that hatred. I never saw in my mother any quality worth emulating. On top of that, the things she did made liking her quite impossible. If I remember right, my mother was plain wicked.

That day, my mother was envious of my sister because I had readily gone with her, and she had, without saying a word, succeeded in bathing me, while my mother, despite her shouting and crying, wasn't able to draw even a word from me. My mother saw this as another victory for my sister, for she did not like to see her own son spending time with her stepdaughter. She had tried every trick in the book to pull me away from my sister but, in the end, my sister always won because in all my mother's attempts at tearing us apart, there was no love for me, there was only the cruel desire to beat my sister. When my sister was bathing me at the well, I saw Yaya standing at the kitchen window. She ground her teeth and shouted all kinds of obscenities at my sister.

My sister ignored her and immediately set about cleaning the kitchen. After cleaning up, she removed the lids from the pots of rice and dal that she had cooked. As soon as the lids were opened, I saw a wave of anger cross my sister's face. Avoiding my sister's gaze, I peered into the pots. Someone had thrown ash from the chulha on the rice and two dead cockroaches in the dal.

My sister seemed to be lost in thought for a while. Then she picked up one dead cockroach by its leg and went straight to the room where my mother was lying on a cot with her left hand on her forehead, covering part of her eyes. My sister tapped my mother's hand. Yaya moved her hand from her forehead. Kako dangled the dead cockroach in front of her eyes. A furious silence lay between my mother and her stepdaughter. Kako then opened her mouth, popped the cockroach in and began chewing it. I had never seen this facet of my sister. I realised that day that my sister was as savage as she was silent.

Yaya got up with a start, burning with rage. She moved her hand to hit my sister, but my sister grabbed her hand mid-air. Yaya tried to free her hand, but my sister's grip was stronger.

'Bitch!' Yaya screamed at Kako. 'You've come to put up a show ...'

Kako did not protest. She kept holding my mother's arm firmly for some time before releasing it. Then, tossing her long, curly hair, like she often did, she spat the chewed cockroach at Yaya's feet, turned around and left the room.

She went to the kitchen, took some water from a pot and rinsed her mouth. She lit the chulha once again. The firewood burned eagerly. It was as if the fire were calling out to raw grains the way hunger calls out to food. Flames seemed to embrace the pot of rice when Kako placed it on the burning chulha. For as long as the union of fire and rice lasted, Kako ground a chilli, coriander leaves, tomato and cucumber on the grinding stone. I absolutely adored that chutney she used to make. That is why she had nicknamed me Chutroo.

She took some cooked rice, mixed it with the chutney and fed me the first morsel of food I'd had in days. Yaya stood behind her, threatening me with her eyes. Ignoring her, I opened my mouth and took the food from my sister's hand. After I had swallowed that first serving, I picked up some rice, mixed it with the chutney, and brought it close to my sister's mouth. She smiled, opened her mouth, and ate the rice I fed her.

After our meal, we went to our room. Kako spread a mat on the floor and made me lie down beside her. She stroked my hair, and I slept for hours, my head resting on her right arm.

I got up in the late afternoon. I saw Yaya in the yard, picking red amaranth leaves for cooking, and Kako milking the cow in the shed. The cow lifted her muzzle, covered with straw, ruminated while looking at me for some time, then put her mouth again in the manger. The redness of the setting sun shone on Kako's hair; some of it fell on her dusky face. I went to her and she embraced me with her left arm while continuing to milk the cow with her right. It isn't easy to milk the two udders of a cow with one hand, but my sister was adept at doing that. While the entire village admired this skill of hers, my mother envied her.

That afternoon, too, Yaya looked at us from the corner of her eyes. I was just ten years old at the time, so I could not understand my mother's hatred. It was only when I grew older that I learnt how dirty her thoughts were about the relationship my sister and I shared. She treated our relationship like something illicit, something immoral.

I placed my chin on my sister's shoulder and looked intently at the pot into which two streams of milk fell. They created froth as they fell, setting up a steady hum as they hit the pool of milk. That hum of falling milk touched every corner of the shed. My sister's silence, though, stood out. I had no idea then that it held within itself an explosive.

My sister raised me prudently and resiliently, and enabled me to achieve something in life. But then she left this life to join a different one, a dangerous one.

My sister was usually quiet. Even with me, she was often brusque. Most of the time, her quavering breath was sufficient to tell me what was on her mind. I had believed that I would spend the rest of my life under my sister's care and guidance, but I was wrong. My sister's life took a different direction and, with that, there came a distance between me and my Adivasi village, Basamura.

It was my sister who paved the path for me to venture out of my Adivasi village and attain that most powerful of means: education. She left no stone unturned to educate me till the intermediate level. She cut firewood and gathered tendu leaves in the forest. She sold tree sap, honey, mahua flowers and fruits, wood apples, jamun, jujubes, mangoes, and even fish, junglefowl, partridges and quails. I loved jamuns, their tart flavour and their fragrance, and my sister took care to pick the best ones for me. Whatever money she earned from selling produce from the forest, she invested it in my education. And she fought anyone who came between her and her objective, be it a wild animal or an officer in the forest department.

I never understood why my sister left the village and retired to the depths of the forest after pushing me out into *civilisation.* She herself turned into a forest—mysterious and frightening. A deep, endless forest, where trees and bushes created a maze, and where, at every turn, lurked my sister's fears and insecurities.

## CHAPTER 4

# Silence

My sister was twenty-seven when I turned twenty. She never married; she chose the forest as her consort. I was studying in the engineering college in Raipur at the time. I lived in the Adivasi Hostel, the hostel meant only for Adivasi students. I was preparing for the final paper of the final year when an acquaintance from the village informed me: 'Your sister has left home. She has gone into the forest with Dada Log.'

Dada Log. Literally: Elder Brothers. Whom the world outside knew as Naxalites.

After writing down the answer to the last question of the test, I left the exam centre immediately and went straight to the bus stand. I took the bus which would drop me at a dirt track about three kilometres from my village.

Like other Adivasi villages in the area, Basamura too did not have a bus stop. There was only a tin plate hung or tied somewhere by the road outside a village. On that tin plate would be written the name of that particular village. The tin plate marked the spot where buses stopped for passengers from the village to alight or climb aboard before they resumed their journey.

On those tin plates, beneath the name of a village, there usually was an arrow pointing towards a dirt track that led to the village.

I got down on the big road, beside the tin plate bearing the name 'Basamura' and followed the track that would take me to my village. There was another track there, which went into the forest—the track that I had taken to go after the elephant, the track that my sister too had taken, once she left home. As I walked, I wondered how the tracks came to be made. How many people must have taken a particular route for it to become a track? And how much trust there must have been for all of them to take that same route? The person who must have been the first to walk on a certain route perhaps did not know that they were not merely walking on a route—they were creating a landmark, they were creating a track for posterity.

I stopped all of a sudden, quite taken aback by the fact that I was thinking of something so irrelevant—about tracks and how they came to be—instead of focusing on reaching home quickly. I had travelled 120 kilometres from the city to my village to find out about my sister, but instead of my sister, my mind was filled with nonsensical stuff like tracks and routes!

I shook my head, as if trying to throw 'tracks' out of it, and tried to focus on my sister. Perhaps there wasn't very much to think about her walking into the depths of the forest. I'd never seen the 'Dada Log' whom the acquaintance had mentioned, but I was aware of my sister's links with them. I knew that she was secretly connected with those people. No one else knew that. Only I knew.

But now that my sister's connection with the Dada Log had been revealed, I only wanted to know what the villagers—who used to admire my sister—thought about her now and if my sister had left any message for me.

I came across several acquaintances on the path, but they all treated me like a stranger, as if they did not know me. It was clear that they were trying to avoid me, for they were afraid, and for a good reason—that being seen with me would land them in trouble.

I saw Soyam Rama coming on a bicycle. Rama was my cousin, the son of my father's sister. I waved at him to stop, but he too pretended not to have seen me and tried to pass by quickly. I grabbed the pannier rack of his bicycle. He hurriedly put his left foot on the ground to balance himself and, turning around, annoyed, shouted an expletive at me. I did not mind.

'Where are you going?' I asked Rama.

'Till the bus stop,' Rama said.

'Why? Is it important work?'

'No. Nothing much. Just going to buy some beedi for my father.'

'Come. I need to talk to you.'

I held the handle of his bicycle and pulled it under a tamarind tree a little away from the track. Rama was so anxious and visibly scared he didn't even alight from the bicycle. His right leg was still hanging across the top tube while he hobbled on his left leg as I pulled the bicycle away from the track. His breathing had turned uneven and he was nearly gasping.

'Where is Irma Kako?' I looked him in the eye and asked.

'She—she has left home.'

'Why? With whom?'

'Don't know—I don't know.'

'You don't know or you don't want to tell?'

Rama lowered his head and stood in the same position—left foot on the ground, right leg dangling across the top tube—for some time. He said nothing. Then he straightened his body, placed his right foot on the pedal and tried to release the handle from my grasp.

I grabbed his collar from the back.

'What were the villagers saying when she left the village with Dada Log?' I asked.

Rama gave me a helpless glance.

'Everyone in the village is frightened,' he managed to utter. 'No one is saying anything.'

I could see that Rama himself was very frightened. I released the handle of the bicycle. That was the moment Rama had been waiting for. He pressed his right foot on the pedal, somehow balanced himself, and raced the bicycle to the track. Once on the track, he looked neither left nor right. He just cycled away as fast as he could towards the bus stop, away from me. I watched him go, then I turned around and resumed walking towards the village.

Jogi Oyami, our neighbour, was pulling out weeds in his field. On spotting me, he immediately looked away. At the centre of the village, where I'd seen the elephant ten years ago, some villagers sat under a peepul tree. They all eyed me suspiciously. When I turned towards the alley that led to my house, the women sitting or working outside their homes avoided me completely. No one spoke to me. Even the children playing on the street ran away upon seeing me, as if I were some frightful animal that had broken into their space.

But, it wasn't fear that I saw on their faces. Yes, it was something like fear. But more than fear, it was worry. Worry that they would land in trouble because of me.

I had already guessed what would happen at home. Yaya started shouting dirty expletives the moment she saw me approaching. I had nothing to say. Yaya was accusing me of keeping things hidden. She was accusing Kako and me equally of having besmirched the honour of the family. And, as was her wont, she came straight down to accusing us of having a physical relationship. All that I could still handle. But when Yaya started describing the genitalia of my sister, I knew I'd had enough. I turned red with anger and pressed my hand upon her mouth, and kept it pressed till she started gagging.

Buba sat quietly on one side. It was unbelievable that a short-tempered man like him, who was prone to violence at the drop of a hat, could sit so quietly. What was the secret of this quiet?

I moved Yaya aside and walked towards my father. To my surprise, he looked afraid of me. He started moving away from me. He grabbed his stick that stood against the wall, but it was no longer his weapon. It had turned into a means of self-defence. I couldn't understand why he needed to defend himself from me. I stared at him, trying to read what was going on in his mind. I saw that he was sweating profusely and couldn't look me in the eye. Something told me that his wickedness had a hand in my sister's departure.

Yaya had started wailing, and pretty loudly. There was no sorrow or remorse in that wailing. It was just a devious ruse to attract attention. My uncle came rushing. As soon as he saw me, he started to say something—perhaps something dirty about my sister and me. I blocked his face with my palm. He said nothing.

I walked into the room my sister and I had shared before I went away to the city.

I unlocked the tin box in which my clothes were kept. There was nothing there that seemed like a message from my sister. Then I looked at the clothes horse upon which she usually left something for me. That too did not have anything for me. I sighed deeply. For the first time in my life, I felt as if I had been left all alone.

When I stepped outside, I saw that a crowd had gathered. A crowd that was curious to know a secret, if there was one. I ignored everyone and hiked to the point from where one path went into the forest and the other towards the road to the city. It was the same point from where, ten years ago, mesmerised by the elephant, I had followed it into the forest.

I had no desire anymore to talk to anyone or know anything from anyone. I stood there for a long time. I could have gone searching for my sister had she been missing. Point is: she wasn't lost, she hadn't gone missing. My sister had left. She hadn't left any message for me. She had just left. Just like that. Just the way that mahout had left me, alone, in the forest, sitting atop the elephant, ten years ago.

Why did the mahout leave me and go away? That was still a mystery to me. And equally mysterious was my sister who—after having raised me, educated me and enabled me to make my own way in this world—had left me.

What should I do now? Which path should I choose? Questions were jostling within me, threatening to break loose. When I couldn't arrive at a decision, I picked up two stones from the ground. One was black and flat; the other was white and round. I threw the flat one towards the forest and the round one towards the road leading away from my village. The flat stone hit a branch of a tree close by and fell on the ground. The round one rolled quite far down the path from the village.

I had made my decision. I decided that I would follow the stone that would go farther. I walked out of my village. It isn't easy—perhaps it isn't possible—for a human to choose their destiny. But they could certainly make a spontaneous choice, for that particular time. I had made my choice. I saw the villagers watching me as I picked up the round stone and walked away.

That stone is still safe with me. I am not superstitious about the stone the way the villagers are about their deities and shrines. But the stone had helped me make a choice, a decision, and I came to see it as the only memento I had left of my sister. The villagers had their deities and superstitions and ancient patriarchal beliefs to hold on to. I had none of those. And my sister too had left me nothing. I had nothing except the memories of my sister and her silence; and that round, white stone.

Some time later, I named my sister Khamoshi—Silence. And I named that round, white stone Junoon—Passion. It is passion that shows us a path and enables us to clear it. Well-made plans sometimes fail, but passion doesn't fail. Passion always gets us somewhere, no matter the circumstance.

I used that stone named Passion several times and it always gave me an answer, always helped me make a decision. It never failed to inspire me to move forward fearlessly on unknown paths.

## CHAPTER 5

# Ship

The four years of my engineering course were over. Two months after the final exam, my degree was in my hands, and I sat holding it on a bench in the college campus. I was all alone. The rest of the students had collected their degrees and left. I looked around intently, just like that mahout who had, years ago, climbed atop a banyan tree inside a forest and looked in all directions, searching for a way out. He hadn't been able to find one. I had several paths open before me. But if one doesn't know where they intend to go, having several paths open is akin to having no path open to them. I had realised that it wasn't always good sense that helped one to choose a path. Sometimes, it was just chance.

An hour or so later, I found myself sitting on a granite-topped bench at the railway station with all my luggage. I was reading the railway timetable on the wall before me, the names of all the trains that passed through the station. My hand was in my pocket, fiddling with the round stone as one would fiddle with the beads in a rosary.

It was almost quarter to three in the afternoon. A young man, around my age, came and sat beside me on the bench. He had on a cap and a pair of sunglasses. An airbag hung from his shoulder and a heavy backpack on his back.

He dropped his backpack near my suitcase and, like an old friend, patted me on my shoulder. I was quite surprised. He smiled at me and asked, 'What? You can't recognise me?'

He took off his cap and sunglasses, and I saw that he indeed was my friend. Dhananjay, my batchmate.

He exuded such warmth that my fingers stopped fiddling with the round stone and, taking my hand out of my pocket, I extended it towards him.

'Where are you off to?' Dhananjay asked.

'Nowhere.' I smiled, for I really had no idea where I intended to go.

'Good,' he smiled back. 'I guess it's better to go somewhere.'

I nodded.

'Right,' I said. 'I think I have come to the station just to go anywhere and nowhere in particular.'

Dhananjay looked at me, as if trying to make head or tail of what I was saying.

'Tell me,' I said, more to distract Dhananjay from examining my face that way, 'where are you going?'

'I am going to Mumbai,' he said.

'For some work or just like that?'

'I am going to do post-graduation at the L.B.S. Nautical College,' Dhananjay informed me. 'After I pass, I will be eligible to join as an engineer on a ship.'

'Ship!'

My reaction was spontaneous. I had only heard that ships were huge. I had never imagined how big a ship could be. But that day, after hearing Dhananjay mention a ship while sitting on a granite-topped bench at a railway station, our luggage lying around us, the same curiosity that had gripped me when I encountered the elephant all those years ago, took hold of me again. I felt the same strangeness race through me as when I saw an elephant for the first time in my life.

'Can I come with you?' I blurted.

'Of course,' Dhananjay replied readily. 'Who knows, we may both be selected together!'

'That'd be great!' I jumped up. 'I'll go with you.'

I dashed to the booking window to buy a ticket to Mumbai.

Watching me stand in the queue at the booking window, Dhananjay perhaps thought that I was going with him to seek a livelihood. He did not know that I was going to experience something big, once again, the way I had ventured out of my village to experience an elephant at close quarters. He did not know that my destiny wasn't pulling me towards a livelihood, it was pulling me towards something big.

And that was exactly what happened.

L.B.S. Nautical College or Lal Bahadur Shastri Nautical College was named after Lal Bahadur Shastri, the former prime minister of India. After gaining admission there, we were taken to a training ship. I was stunned to see how huge the ship was. Once inside, the expansive machinery made my heart race. Dhananjay was a serious student. He listened attentively to the senior engineer who was delivering the day's lecture and took notes. I looked at Dhananjay and was filled with immense gratitude—after all, I was at a nautical college because of him. It was he who showed me the path to a ship. In the midst of the machinery's din, I grew so emotional I held Dhananjay's hand.

'What happened?' Dhananjay asked. 'Why do you look worried?'

I breathed in hard to keep the tears from welling up. I squeezed his hand a bit and said, 'Thank you.' Dhananjay smiled and squeezed my hand in return. We held hands throughout the class. We roamed through the inside of the ship, climbed staircases and went on the deck, holding hands all the while.

The day was very sunny, and quite windy. Coconut trees were swaying on the seashore. An odorous humidity rose from the rocky shore of Madh Island. My heart was brimming with gratitude and brotherly affection for Dhananjay.

'Dhananjay, I am very grateful to you,' I said, as Dhananjay and I stood against the railing on the deck of the ship. 'I cannot tell you how happy I am in this place.'

'You don't seem yourself,' Dhananjay said. 'What has got you so excited? Tell me.'

'I have this problem,' I tried explaining my situation to Dhananjay. 'I get very excited upon seeing something huge. I'm just taken by large objects. I had never thought that the inside of a ship would be far bigger than my imagination.'

'Brother, look,' Dhananjay said, 'we're still on a training ship. In the next few days, we'll be on an actual ship, floating on the sea. If you are so excited seeing a training ship anchored at the shore, what will you do when boarding an actual, working ship? A running ship will be four times the size of this training ship and the sea three times bigger than land!'

'No worries. I'll see to that. With you by my side, I'll learn everything.' I placed my hands on Dhananjay's shoulders.

Dhananjay too placed his hand on my shoulder, smiling at me, and we left the deck together.

'Do you know why I chose to study marine engineering?' Dhananjay asked me as we went down the stairs.

I looked at him with curiosity.

'Just the way you are mesmerised by huge objects and wide expanses, I am drawn to depths.'

Dhananjay removed his hand from my shoulder. We were standing in front of the engine room. 'Everything that is beneath the surface attracts me. The fathomless depths draw me towards them. When I look into the depths, I get just as excited as you were a while ago.'

'My god!' I rubbed my head in astonishment. 'Then it is not safe to travel with you on a ship.'

'Why? Why do you think so?' Dhananjay's eyes went wide in amazement.

'Because while trying to fathom the deep sea, you may sink the ship.'

Dhananjay laughed.

'Of course,' he said, shaking his head. 'If you take the ship too far, looking for a wide expanse, I will certainly go ahead and sink it.'

'Fine,' I laughed. 'You don't let me wander off, and I won't let you sink.'

'Yaar, it's better to sink once than to keep wandering one's entire life.'

'And if you sink and still don't find what you're looking for?'

'And where will you go when you are tired of wandering?'

'Wanderers do find their shore someday.'

'Those who sink too find something to rest their feet upon.'

Dhananjay's reply stumped me a little bit. I wasn't able to think of a repartee.

He put his arm around my shoulder again and said, 'Enough of sinking and wandering. I'm hungry. Let's go eat something.'

We got off the ship and walked towards the canteen.

CHAPTER 6

# Sea

Dhananjay and I spent the rest of our training together, but we didn't get to work together on a running ship. He used his personal contacts to get me a job in a merchant navy firm, Grand Eastern Shipping Company, while he himself chose the path of submarine engineering, to work in the depths of the ocean.

I boarded MV Jaldoot and set sail from Mumbai to Taiwan, while Dhananjay boarded a submarine and went down into the depths of the sea. Our physical contact was lost, but perhaps we were still in touch through the ocean. The waves held us both together.

My first job was my first sea journey as well. The machinery of a running ship was bigger and more complex than that of a training ship, so I had to handle it patiently. I tried to place myself in all that buzz and friction in the same way one places flowers on an altar. I was to be at sea for six months, but I did not give that much thought. I had been given warnings and suggestions, but I tried not to be too intimidated. I worked quietly in the engine room. Our chief engineer, Mr Shafi, patted my shoulder after my shift was over, praising my work. I thanked him and went straight to the deck from the engine room. I passed a long row of cargo loaded on the deck and reached the bow of the ship.

The bow was where I wanted to be. The vast expanse lay before me. The sea was too mesmerising for words. I held the railing tightly and stared at the horizon where the sea and the sky met, painted in the glow of the setting sun. The waves hitting the ship seemed to be dancing beneath. I should have been happy, very happy. But I wasn't. I felt very lonely and detached. I shut my eyes.

I can't say when the sound of waves turned into the sound of leaves rustling. Leaves in the forest. I followed the sound and it took me to that point outside my village from where one path went into the forest and the other led to the road that took one away from the village and into the city. How many thousands of kilometres away had I come! From my village to far out on the sea!

Why did that sound of leaves rustling play in my ears then? Why did those memories return to me? I was agitated and my hand reached into my pocket, to that stone named Passion. I started rotating Passion between my fingers and the forest flashed before my eyes. It was the same lonely, moonlit night. But, instead of animals, I saw a row of young men and women, all wearing similar guerrilla fatigues, guns slung from their shoulders. They walked quietly, briskly, one after the other, in a disciplined manner. They passed through my vision and

I watched the last person in that row. She was a woman. She had curly hair. I knew that hair. She did not turn around. She walked away, just like the others. But I kept watching her till she disappeared into the unknown depths of the forest.

I knew she was my sister. I knew I could have willed myself to see her face had I only pressed on the stone a bit harder. But no. I did not want to see her face. In no manifestation was I in a position to look into the eyes of my sister.

I took my hand out of my pocket and held the railing with both my hands. The wind had turned stronger and the waves in the sea seemed to leap up. Some moments later, those leaping waves engulfed the sun and pulled it down into the depths of the sea. Gradually, the light followed the sun and disappeared somewhere in the sky. Night had fallen.

I left the deck when it was completely dark. The aroma of dinner floated from the dining hall. I entered to find the place already full. It was our first journey on that ship, so a variety of cuisines had been prepared to welcome us on board. Snacks, soups and drinks were placed on the central dining table. Everyone filled their glasses. Captain Alok Datt greeted everyone. 'We're all together for six months!' he said, and raised his glass in the air. All the employees of the ship responded by raising their glasses together and saying in unison, 'Cheers!'

After the toast, the various departments of the ship separated into groups of their own. Mr Shafi went to one side of the dining hall with his two assistants. The drivers were clinking their glasses together on another side. Waiters, sanitation staff, motormen, wiremen and plumbers flocked together, having a merry time.

I slid towards a dimly lit part of the dining hall and stood there. I felt quite out of place in that noisy gathering. I didn't have a complex; I just found it difficult to mix easily with people whom I had just met.

I looked around the gathering and spotted Captain Alok Datt standing, like me, alone in another dimly lit part of the dining hall and—I froze when I noticed it—staring at me! He wasn't judging me. He was just watching me standing, like him, alone. But his gaze on me was enough to make me feel self-conscious. I averted my gaze. A while later, on the pretext of scratching my head, I again looked in his direction. He wasn't there. Instead, making space between groups of men, he was headed towards me. I was so stunned I couldn't even extend my hand to greet him. I was able to extend it only when he stretched his hand towards me.

There was something in his demeanour that I found agreeable. He led me to the central dining table, prepared a drink each for us, handed me my glass, and then led me to another corner where there was a table by a window.

We sat down, facing each other. He touched his glass against mine and took a large gulp.

'Tradition warrants that we speak with each other,' he said, smiling.

I said nothing. I didn't even smile back. But he kept smiling.

'Are you trying to look for a topic or an excuse?' he asked.

'No,' I said. 'I don't think I'd need an excuse to talk to you.'

'I guessed right. You are one of those people who are not part of a crowd but who believe in stating their thoughts clearly. Also, you are one of those people who speak mostly with their eyes.'

'I think I'm lucky that my eyes are able to speak,' I answered. 'There are people who do not let even their eyes speak.'

Captain Alok Datt wiped his moustache with a napkin and looked at me. It was as if my words had hinted at his own nature.

'Anyway—' He tried to deflect the attention from himself.

'Were it only for a few days, or even a week or two, it wouldn't matter' Captain Alok Datt continued. 'But this is a six-month journey. A journey so long can be damaging to a person like you who is lost in his thoughts.'

I studied his face closely.

'You need not be intimidated by me.' He smiled and patted my shoulder. 'You may feel uneasy for a few days. It takes time to get used to the sea. For a few days, you will be nostalgic for home and all that you've left behind. But after that, the sea will teach you to push all your thoughts and memories ashore.'

I placed my elbows on the table and rested my chin on my palms as I listened to Captain Datt. It wasn't the voice of a sailor. It was the voice of a man who had gone through something, who had spent some time suspended between life and death, or who had—perhaps in an accident—lost that part of his being that produces sympathy, that part which makes humans human.

'Sir, you are right,' I said, when Captain Alok Datt paused for some time. 'When we've given ourselves to the sea, is there any use being attached to objects and memories that we've left behind on land?'

'It is difficult.' Captain Alok Datt stroked his thick beard as he spoke. 'The land does not loosen its grip on us that easily.'

He smiled and shook his head.

'Anyway,' he continued, 'there is no use getting entangled in these worries. Be it sea, be it land, in the end, both bore us. And then one day, we start drinking and feel like masturbating. It is difficult to cross the sea without alcohol and masturbation, because a sailor's life involves not only fighting against sea storms but also against one's own feelings. We struggle with complicated machines in the ship's control room, nearly forgetting that the most complicated control room is within us. If we learn to use our tools in the proper way, no emotion can affect our system.'

I did not reply to anything that Captain Datt said after that. He went on speaking; I just went on listening. And this went on until we had finished eating dinner. I was yet to experience most of the things he talked about. I was yet to learn how to live my life. Captain Alok Datt had, on the other hand, lived half his life. Was it so simple for me to understand him?

I came out on the deck and took a deep breath. The dining hall was warm and somewhat suffocating, but there was a lovely breeze blowing on the deck. It was the month of March. The weather was cool. Some employees of the ship were sprawled on chairs lying on the deck. Some of them were asleep. The rocking of the ship had a lulling effect.

I came down from the deck and walked through the corridor to my cabin. I entered and bolted the door behind me. Now there was neither the fathomless sea nor the ship before me.

I changed and lay down on the hard and narrow bed. Some time passed. Then I felt the machines vibrating to their full capacity in the depths of the ship. The ship wasn't rocking anymore, it surged ahead smoothly, as if it wasn't moving over waves in a sea but on a plain road on land. I could hear the rhythmic sound of the pistons, so much so that it seemed as if all Creation was swirling around that sound.

Unable to sleep, I returned to the deck. Containers were piled on top of each other in rows, the piles as tall as skyscrapers. I passed between the rows. We were passing by the coast of Sri Lanka. The long and endless shadows of those containers floated on the ocean. Somewhere between those huge shadows, perhaps there was my shadow too. Tiny, microscopic.

'What's the matter? Are you unable to sleep?'

Captain Alok Datt stood before me, dressed in a night gown that was billowing in the wind like the sail of a yacht.

'Sir ... this is my first night on a ship,' I mumbled, 'so everything is pretty new to me ...'

'Wait,' Captain Alok Datt interrupted. 'It doesn't seem from your face that you're overwhelmed by your surroundings.'

I said nothing.

'What are you thinking?' Captain Alok Datt asked.

'Nothing,' I said. 'I was just looking at the shadow of the ship.'

'Hmm ...' Captain Alok Datt shook his head as he looked at me. 'It happens to everyone initially. When you return home after spending six months on the ship, you will start looking at your house in the same way as you are looking at the ship now. It'll take you some time to get used to your house too.'

Would I really need time to get used to things the way Captain Alok Datt put it? Had I been truthful in my replies to him? After all, hadn't I learnt to live life as 'thought-lessly' as animals? Don't I believe that one should live one's life like an animal? That instead of changing one's situation to suit oneself, one should change oneself according to the situation?

Captain Alok Datt placed his hand on my shoulder and led me away from the deck. I did not look up at him again. He led me as one would lead a drunk or a sick man. We reached the passage after climbing down the stairs and he took me to my cabin. He opened the door for me and I, like a domesticated animal entering its pen, walked inside.

The next day was terribly busy. The generators were acting up. The control room demanded a constant supply of power and we were unable to provide that. We struggled from morning till afternoon and mended the generators, but they were still unable to provide the requisite amount of power. Without it, the ship would not be able to reach the port in Singapore on time.

I was beset with anxiety. The state of the machinery on the ship had nothing to do with my personal ability. Yet, the frenetic way in which I was working with the machines, it seemed as if I alone were responsible for them. Anxious, I grabbed the stone named Passion that lay in my pocket. Within a few moments, I seemed to have an epiphany. I went down to the engine room and began examining the pistons. I realised that their inner ring was broken because of which the generators were having to take up extra load.

I did not tell anyone, nor did I inform my chief. Without giving it another thought, without thinking of the consequences, I went straight to the power station. I pulled all the levers and turned all the generators off. As a result, the ship stopped. I was aware of the protocol; only the captain of the ship had the power to decide if it could be stopped while it was sailing. But, at that juncture, I was driven by Passion and did not think any captain in the world had the power to stop me.

The very next moment, I was surrounded by the drivers and engineers. Mr Shafi, the officer I was supposed to report to, shook me by the shoulders.

'Have you lost your senses?' he boomed.

I looked up at Mr Shafi, and I don't know what he saw on my face or in my eyes, but his grip on my body loosened. I did not bother to look at the other staff surrounding me. I took the electric spanner and moved towards the panel of the pistons. Some workers tried to block my way, but Mr Shafi raised his hand and kept them from stopping me. When I touched the spanner to the bolt of the panel, Mr Shafi placed his hand on my shoulder again and said, 'May I ask what you intend to do now?'

'I intend to do what needs to be done,' I said. Had it been someone other than Mr Shafi, they would have pushed me out of the ship then and there. But Mr Shafi responded in a different way. He squatted with me before the panel, hands on his knees, and bringing his face close to mine, asked me gently, 'Is there any way in which I can help you?'

I now feel that I should have melted with shame then. But I didn't, for I was being driven by Passion. So I gave him a practical and relevant reply, 'The rings of pistons 3, 5 and 6 are broken. They need to be changed quickly.'

Mr Shafi stood up straight, pushed his glasses which had slid down to the bridge of his nose back to his eyes, and scratched his beard for some time. He could have asked me how I knew, without opening the piston block, that the rings were broken. But he didn't. Instead, he called Senior Engineer Sanjay Deshpande, Second Engineer Mukesh Verma and Third Engineer Joginder Singh and explained the situation to them. All three of them nodded in agreement and called over a few technicians. A team was ready and I was its undeclared leader.

We finished fixing the pistons in forty-five minutes. The ship was restarted and gained the required speed in just half an hour. Everyone was happy. But I wasn't. For repairing the machine had been made possible not by my toil or experience but by a stone.

'Your expertise saved us so many hours,' Mr Shafi said, patting my back. Everyone looked at me admiringly.

But there were several questions within me that were making me anxious: Was I nothing without that mystical stone? Would it control my actions all the time? Didn't I have the ability to accomplish something without its assistance? What would happen if, someday, I lost the stone?

Two days later, our ship docked at a port in Singapore. Hundreds of ships from all over the world stood docked to cast-iron ramps like buffaloes tied in rows on a dairy farm.

The entire port was gleaming. It was the shine of brilliance. Of modern cranes and world-class machinery and glass buildings.

I stood on the deck of my ship wondering how humans could be so dwarfed in comparison to the huge structures they created. Agents from import companies scuttled about like busy ants. Labourers in blue overalls, white helmets and canvas shoes, scurried up and down the gangways like tiny insects.

I climbed down the ramp. It had heated up in the sun. The dirty water from the dock, mixed with the diesel and machine oil from the ships' engines, made the space even hotter.

I wiped away my sweat with a handkerchief and walked towards the snacks corner. It was an international cafeteria. I sat down at a table near a wall made of glass and began watching the port, ramps and ships.

Jaldoot, our ship, was docked nearby. I hadn't had the opportunity so far to watch its exterior closely. I hadn't even imagined how its exterior would be. I kept staring at its shiny, black body. It reminded me of the elephant.

I averted my gaze from Jaldoot and began watching the other ships. There was a ship from Brazil, laden with coffee and spices. Next to it was a ship from China, with its cargo of electronic toys and equipment meant for retail markets. There were ships from Malaysia and Indonesia with palm oil. There were other ships too, some carrying coal, some cement and asphalt, others carrying tarpaulin, urea, polyester, equipment and machine parts, bags of grains, powdered milk, fish and meat. After taking a look at all the ships, my gaze stopped on my table where a sandwich and a cup of coffee had arrived.

I stared at the slices of bread and the steaming cup of coffee, thinking of all the work a person had to do and all the places they had to go in order to be able to earn a slice of bread. I wondered what place a man with a sandwich and a cup of coffee in his hands had in this vast cluster of sky-high structures and modern machinery. Then I realised that I was sitting in an international café at an international port and that perhaps I shouldn't be thinking about mundane things like bread and livelihood and the place of an ordinary man.

Troubled by my thoughts, I finished my snack quickly and left the cafeteria to return to my ship. As I walked down the corridor, I saw that all the cabins were empty. Everyone had gone out on a sightseeing tour of Singapore. Only Captain Alok Datt had stayed back on the ship. The door to his cabin was partly open. I peered in and saw him hunched at his desk, writing something in what looked like a diary. I admired his ability to remain focused on work. I turned around quietly and went to my cabin. Once inside, I was engulfed by a sense of annoyance and utter meaninglessness. I threw myself on the bed, covered myself with a sheet and fell asleep.

Singapore had refreshed and invigorated all the workers on MV Jaldoot. I too tried to drown myself in work the next day onwards. I had got used to the engine room. I meant to throw myself into work in order to keep my mind free of lofty ideas that would yield nothing.

The journey from Singapore to Taiwan was pleasant. I had begun to mix freely with my co-workers by now, and my behaviour had turned from purely practical to somewhat gregarious. I came to respect Mr Shafi even more. He used to only offer advice earlier, but now he also started to lovingly chide me from time to time. He would often check if I'd had my meals, as if he were my guardian. I discovered that Senior Engineer Sanjay Deshpande did not have much of a sense of humour, but he did not mind an occasional joke or two. Second Engineer Mukesh Verma was both practical and funny and had this curious habit of keeping photographs of all his ex-girlfriends with him. Third Engineer Joginder Singh did not have too many interesting anecdotes of his own, so he mostly listened.

I was the youngest on the team, so I kept a respectful distance from them. I would join in their conversations, but I did not participate actively because I was aware of my place. Also, I wasn't adept at socialising and did not have any experience impressive enough to be shared. Mr Shafi made me tag along with him most of the time and tried his best to smarten me up. He was from Lucknow and had a distinctive style of expressing himself. He talked of the traditions in his family and of days gone by. My other co-workers too had memories of their families and of the lives they had lived so far.

What did I have? Which lineage and which family could I have spoken of? The place I came from was still a long way from *civilisation*. In the place I came from, a person was yet to be considered human.

I had been able to bridge the gap between that world and this and had landed on this ship. I too wasn't *civilised*, but I had managed to cross over to this arena of global trade. Wasn't I like an ape who had been picked from a forest in one ecological zone and transported far away to a different zone altogether? I had walked out of my village along a dirt track and reached one of the busiest sea ports in the world. Was there a logical reasoning behind this? Why did I come here? What was I doing here? Would I ever be able to connect with this life? Or was I destined to remain under some sort of spell? The spell cast by an elephant, the spell cast by this ship.

I was standing on the deck one night, eyeing my future suspiciously, wondering what the purpose of my existence was and what lay in store for me, when I felt a hand on my shoulder. I knew that hand. It extended around my shoulder and led me down the corridor to my cabin. Then it opened the door of the cabin for me. But that night, I did not enter my cabin like a tame animal. I turned around and looked into Captain Alok Datt's eyes. I wanted to know what was inside that man, how many worlds, how many secrets.

Just a few nights ago, I'd seen Captain Datt on the deck. I had returned silently to my cabin. But unable to sleep, I'd returned to the deck nearly four hours later. Captain Datt was still standing there, holding the railing, just the way I had left him. Alarmed, I went and touched him on the shoulder. He turned around, and I saw in his eyes the same lack of thought that one would see in the eyes of an animal. I immediately averted my gaze. I didn't want him to sense that I had seen something in his eyes.

That day, outside my cabin, when I looked into Captain Datt's eyes, it was he who averted his gaze and walked away.

The next morning, at breakfast, Captain Alok Datt avoided me. I saw him grow anxious and bark insensible orders to his juniors. I thought it better to move out of his way.

There was something between us, between Captain Datt and me. I had sensed it long back. We came from disparate backgrounds. There was a big age gap between us. Despite that, it seemed as if we were looking out for each other. It was very mysterious. When I spent the nights on the deck, sad, thoughtful, Captain Datt would hold me and lead me to my cabin. It never bothered him that I was merely a third engineer on the ship while he was its captain.

Captain Datt did bring me back to my cabin, but I think he was unaware that I did not immediately go to bed. After some time, I returned to the deck, only to find him standing there, holding the railing, staring into the dark distance.

While on the deck at night, Captain Datt wasn't lost in thought all the time. He appeared to be intently observing something playing on the surface of the ocean. For he swung back sometimes; sometimes he moved away from the railing, as if frightened by something. Sometimes he ran and hid behind the stacks of containers. Sometimes he did not return to the railing and observed the sea while hiding behind the containers.

But he wasn't frightened all the time. Sometimes he turned aggressive. Sometimes he looked plain angry. He would march ahead and punch the railing. Sometimes he walked dejectedly in circles, sighing deeply.

I don't think anyone other than me had seen Captain Datt on the deck in the small hours. After I saw that emotionless, animal-like thing in his eyes, I did not dare to walk up to him. I would just watch him from afar.

Six months later, our ship returned to the port in Mumbai after having travelled to Singapore, Taiwan, Japan, Malaysia and Indonesia. In those six months, all of us humans on the ship had become as jaded as the cargo we transported. Returning to land after six months on the sea was like waking up from a nightmare. Somehow, the sea, despite being real, felt like a meaningless fantasy. Setting foot on the ground felt starkly real.

I went with my colleagues from the port to the C.S.T. railway station. They had returned to becoming human after living as cargo for six months. Their happiness showed on their faces. The moment they entered the mobile coverage area, they began calling their families. They kissed their children, and expressed love for their wives and respect for their parents, all through their mobile phones.

Sitting, once again, on a bench in the railway station, I saw scenes from the family lives of other people with the detachment of someone who either does not have a family or whose family has broken apart. It felt just like four years ago, when I was at the railway station in Raipur—neither was I in a hurry to go anywhere, nor did I have anywhere to go till Dhananjay showed me a path.

The train brought me from C.S.T. in Mumbai to the railway station in Raipur. The town had undergone some changes in the four years that I had been away. A gallery had been built along the footpath on the road, and in that gallery, there were plants and handicrafts prepared by Adivasi artisans. There were terracotta murals depicting Adivasi life on the walls, and just opposite that government-sponsored display, there were, on the other side of the road, showrooms of big companies and brands. Adivasi life on one side, the modern marketplace on the other. Terracotta murals on one side, digital signboards on the other.

I was able to see all these changes because I was travelling on a pedal-operated cycle rickshaw. Had I travelled in an auto rickshaw, all those changes would have flown by unnoticed very quickly. The relaxed, rickety gait of a cycle rickshaw enabled me to see the city clearly. I saw that half the city was in a hurry to get ahead with its ambitions and multiplexes, while the other half was still entangled in its crowded dwellings, encroachments, temples dedicated to Bajrangbali, and mazaars built to cause obstruction.

Had these changes crossed over to the villages too? I wondered. The cycle rickshaw brought me to the bus stand and I boarded a bus that would take me to Basamura, my village. I was neither happy nor eager to return to my village, but when the bus stopped outside Basamura, I got down.

One thing had changed. The dirt track wasn't there anymore. It had been replaced by a paved road. But as I walked ahead, I was taken aback to see that the fields on both sides of the road were filled with weeds, as if they hadn't been tilled for years. There was no one bathing at the pond outside the village. There was no one under the peepul tree in the centre of the village, there was no one filling water at the well. Once in the village, I was received by the biggest shock of all: the doors of most of the houses were either broken or locked from the outside.

Some vehicle honked behind me. I moved away from the path. A Maruti Gypsy passed by. There were policemen in it. A jeep followed the Gypsy, and I saw policemen holding guns sitting in the jeep.

Having been out of touch with the happenings in my village for so many years, I found it hard to understand what the police were doing there. I turned onto the path leading to my house. It was hard to recognise the place, for that wasn't how I had last seen it. Most of the houses in our alley had either been demolished or burnt down. The condition of my house was the same. One of its walls had completely crumbled. The yard was overrun with weeds. One door was broken and there was a huge spiderweb in the gap.

I left my backpack outside the house, cleared the spiderweb and entered the house. I was sorry I did. The house had been abandoned. There were more weeds, dust and spiderwebs inside. The entire attic and the roof had come down, and the ground had been dug up in many places. It looked like a big search operation had been conducted in my house. But I wondered if the house had crumbled before being abandoned or after.

I stood in the shaft of light entering through the broken roof, but I felt nothing for my house. I should have been sad or upset or even startled at seeing, all of a sudden, my house completely fallen down—but nothing. Nothing at all. I just stood there, as emotionless as an animal.

Suddenly, there was the sound of footsteps outside the house. Boots. Several pairs of them. All synchronised. As if it were the military marching past. I went out and saw a dozen or so policemen dressed in khaki fatigues outside my house. My cousin Sukhdev, the son of my mother's sister, was also among them. In fact, he was the one leading the platoon. I looked at the other policemen. More than half of them were from my own village. Each one had a gun in the hand and a badge on the shoulder. On the badge was written: S.P.O.

They stared at me for some time. Then one of them picked up my backpack. Two policemen stepped forward and held me by the arm.

'You've been summoned to the police station,' Sukhdev said. His tone was matter-of-fact, without any preamble or formality.

'Take me there,' I said, in as direct a tone as him.

My directness perhaps unnerved them a bit, for they had expected me to get scared upon hearing the mention of a police station or on seeing their guns. Perhaps they had thought of making a show of grabbing me and dragging me to the police station. I perhaps foiled their plans. Their mechanical movement, like clockwork puppets, made me laugh.

My directness and fearlessness remained even inside the police station. I went straight to the officer and stood before him. It was a big deal for a person from our area to go and stand so fearlessly before a police officer. Whoever was summoned to the police station went either with their hands folded or were pushed or dragged inside by the policemen.

I did not just stand fearlessly before the officer, I extended my hand towards him. It was a spontaneous gesture on my part, not a pretence. But the officer was startled by it.

*'Baithiye,'* the officer said to me in Hindi. *Sit down.*

*'Farmaiye,'* I said in Urdu, as I had learnt from Mr Shafi. *Please tell.*

The officer rubbed his chin for some time, as if looking for a thread to start speaking to me. Then he looked up at me.

'No one here has seen you in the last three-four years,' the officer said to me. 'Where were you all these days? I want to know.'

'I was in Mumbai, studying engineering,' I answered calmly. 'I got a job with a shipping company soon after.'

'Did you tell your family about your education and job?'

'No.'

'Why?'

'I am not attached to my family. Only to my sister, who left home four years ago.'

'So why have you returned after all this time?'

'To meet my sister.'

'Do you know where she is?'

'In the forest.'

'Where in the forest?'

'That I don't know.'

'Then how will you meet her?'

'I am on vacation for six months. I will wander the forest. Maybe I'll find her somewhere.'

'Do you know anything about your sister?'

'I only know that she gave up her ordinary clothing before leaving home and went into the forest with some of her companions.'

'Would you like to give any more information about your sister and her companions?'

'No. I don't know anything about them.'

'Good. Now I find it necessary to inform you that your sister has joined the Naxalite movement and, at present, she is the area commander of this zone.'

'I don't know what the Naxalite movement is, but I respect any decision taken by my sister. I will go into the forest not to meet any area commander but my sister.'

'Look, nearly fifty villages of this area have been gripped by the Naxalite movement. The situation is such that all those villages have been vacated and their inhabitants moved to relief camps.'

'Look,' I spoke in the same tone as the officer, 'I have got nothing to do with any movement. I will go into the forest only to meet my sister.'

'I cannot give you permission to go into the forest.'

'I'm not asking you for permission. I am an Adivasi and I do not need anyone's permission to go into the forest.'

'Look, don't bring your being an Adivasi into this matter. I too am an Adivasi, but things have changed a lot. The situation here is volatile.'

'Please tell me why you have summoned me here. What do you want from me?'

For some time, the officer kept looking at my face, as if thinking of ways to show me my place. But however hard he tried, he could not bring to his face the kind of cruelty that comes not from mere training or arrogance but from a hatred for the Other. The officer was an Adivasi—an Other, basically—so he lacked hatred.

'I summoned you to inform you that it is my duty to monitor the family members and relatives of all those people who have joined the Naxalite movement. If you want to stay in this area, you will have to mark attendance in the police station every twenty-four hours.'

'Thank you for the information.' I stood up. 'I will try to not hinder your duty. Please allow me to leave now. And please hand me my belongings.'

While the officer and I were talking, my bag had been emptied and all its contents laid neatly on the table between the officer and me. Clothes, sheets, towel and underwear on one side, and soap, toothpaste, toothbrush, oil and comb on the other side. Along with these, all my documents, certificates, ID card and papers related to my employment in the merchant navy too had been placed on the table. Also, that stone called Passion—that too was placed near the edge of the table.

The officer bent over the table and went through my documents. He said to me, 'These papers will be sent to headquarters to be examined.'

'That's fine,' I said.

'Return his things,' the officer ordered Sukhdev.

Sukhdev packed my belongings in my bag and handed it to me.

'There's one more object on your table that belongs to me,' I said to the officer. 'You may examine that too.'

'What object?' The officer was surprised.

I pointed towards the stone.

The officer stared at the stone for some time, then he asked me, 'What is this?'

'You may see for yourself,' I said. 'You have the authority.'

The officer glared at me and said quite bitterly, 'I've been kind to you. I haven't yet behaved with you like an officer. You too behave like a responsible citizen. Don't talk in riddles.'

I nodded my head respectfully and said, 'This isn't about my citizenship, nor is it about the type of stone. It's just that this stone is almost a life vision device for me.'

My words turned that officer grave. It was as if I had revealed the location of a stash of contraband weapons. He looked at the stone intently, perhaps suspiciously.

I picked up the stone, brought it close to his eyes and said to him, 'Look at this stone carefully. If you are really an Adivasi and the government hasn't been able to turn you yet, you'll be able to see a vision in this stone. You will be able to see all your kin, with axe, hatchet, bow and arrows and spear in their hands. You will be able to see your entire community that has now been divided into two. Half of them have donned guerrilla fatigues and gone into the forest, and the other half has, like you, donned this khaki uniform given by the government. But both halves have given up our traditional weapons and picked up guns to stand against each other.'

The officer stood up hastily, as if a snake or a scorpion had got into his clothes and stung him. I put the stone in my pocket, grabbed my bag and walked out of the police station. The officer stared, dumbfounded, as I left.

## CHAPTER 7

# Statue

After stepping out of the police station, I walked briskly towards that point where there were two tracks: one, towards the road that took one from the village to the city, and the other that led to the forest. I did not think twice about choosing a path. I took the one that went into the forest.

I found a barrier and a check post a little ahead. There were two policemen at the check post, standing behind stacks of sacks filled with sand, their machine guns positioned over them. Another policeman was talking on a wireless set. There were two more policemen, one on either side of the barrier. They were alerted by my arrival. The policeman who had been talking on the wireless stepped out of the cabin and eyed me suspiciously. It was clear that he was being informed about me on the wireless. When he had confirmed—looking at my built and appearance—that the person he had been informed about was me, he instructed a policeman at the barrier to lift it and let me pass.

While passing through the barrier, I looked at the policeman who had lifted the barrier. He seemed familiar. I turned around and took another look. Yes, he was Ronhu, who had studied with me till primary school. We used to tease him so much that he often ended up crying and thus we nicknamed him Ronhu, the cry baby. I remembered that he grew up to be quite cowardly and cried at the drop of a hat till the age of seventeen or eighteen. I wondered how a cowardly fellow like him had got a job in the police.

Along with Ronhu, the faces of several of my relatives and schoolmates flashed in my memory. As I began entering the depths of the forest, I encountered several familiar faces. The men were all dressed in police uniforms and patrolling the area. Every hundred feet or so, I saw a policeman strolling with a gun in his hands. They all looked at me strangely as I passed them by, as if they were not watching a human but an alien from outer space. I spotted my cousins—sons of my father's sisters and my mother's brothers—and also my best friend from childhood, Punuram, among the policemen. I thought they recognised me, but they soon turned and walked ahead like strangers.

I did not talk to them. I did not ask them about my sister. I just passed them by like they did not exist, on that path or in the forest.

The path now began curving and sloping up. I turned around the first and the second curves quite easily. But I panted through my climb up the third curve. I stopped to catch my breath after I had turned.

When I was relaxed enough, I noticed that there were, on my right, a row of short statues. I wondered who had erected them in the middle of the forest, and why. They were made of cement and they were all shown holding guns in their hands. Black boots made of cement, khaki uniform made of cement, cement guns in cement hands, and cement helmets on cement heads. It was clear from the guns that these statues were of men who had been recruited by the government as S.P.O.—Special Police Officers—to counter the Naxalites but who had been killed at their hands. The statues stood proudly, despite their plaster having chipped and fallen off at a few places.

I went closer and noticed that they stood on separate plinths of their own. On each plinth was affixed a marble plaque mentioning the word *shaheed*—martyr—before the name of the person and their dates of birth and death. There were a few martyrs whose statues had partly crumbled as they had been built with less cement and more sand. Half of a hand of one particular statue had crumbled; on another, the entire gun had crumbled.

The first statue was that of Soyam Narwa, the son of my neighbour Soyam Ganga. Narwa had liked to hunt quail and partridge and rear poultry right from his childhood. So engrossed was he in his hobbies that he hardly helped around the house. Nearly everyday, from his childhood till his adolescence, he used to be thrashed by his father. The daily beatings made him so stubborn that one day his father too got tired of beating him. Later on, I remember, Narwa did nothing except attend cockfights at the haat and drink liquor distilled from Mahua flowers.

The second statue was that of my cousin, Madavi Budraiya, the son of my father's brother Madavi Ayit. Budraiya was known all over the village by his nickname Chuchru. He was such a stay-at-home that it was impossible to see him outside the house except at sunrise and sunset when he went to empty his bowels. He occasionally went outside on an errand or two, but that too was quite rare. He had an idiotic look on his face, always kept sucking his thumb, and readily ate whatever he was given. My uncle was quite sharp and belligerent, ready to pick a fight at the drop of a hat. So his son's idiocy and the habit of sucking his thumb bothered him a lot. One day, he started beating Chuchru with the whip used to hit bullocks. Chuchru neither screamed nor cried—he just started foaming at the mouth. That day onwards, Chuchru was left to his fate. I wondered who had recruited Chuchru as an S.P.O. Or had he been recruited at all?

The third statue was that of my cousin, Sodi Adama, the son of my mother's brother Sodi Budhra. The relationship between my family and my mother's family was strained, mainly because of the greedy and sly nature of my father. My mother's brother did not like him at all. Our families hardly met, and I got to meet Adama only at the haat or some social gathering. He was an earnest boy, hardworking and truthful. He never loitered or wasted time at the haat. He came there to sell the fish he caught from his pond or the vegetables and watercress he grew on his farm. He was very careful with money, but he did treat me to tea and bhujiya.

I could not recognise the fourth, the fifth and the sixth statues. Perhaps the men were not known to me. But upon reading their surnames on the plaque, I could tell that they were related to one another.

The seventh statue was that of the son of the headman of my village. He was quite a crook. Bullying others, snatching money and other valuables like poultry from people, grabbing the hands of young girls at the market—these were the things the fellow used to do. At the mere age of twenty, he had fathered three children from three different women—illicit children, for he never owned up to being their father. Clearly, to become an S.P.O., one need not have morals or even a strong character.

So much of the plaster from the eighth statue had fallen off that the iron bars inside the structure were visible. I couldn't identify in whose image the statue had been made, but was stunned on reading the person's name on the marble plaque. It was the statue of Buba, my father! What surprised me was not my father's statue but the fact that somebody had deemed it fit to call that useless man—even if he were an S.P.O.—a martyr! I was so repulsed that I walked ahead without casting a glance at the ninth statue.

After taking a few steps, I stopped. I felt as if there was some connection between me and the ninth statue, which I had left unseen. Something told me that I should turn around and look at it.

As I walked back, I felt a mysterious silence fall upon the entire forest. Not one leaf moved. I couldn't tell why I was drawn towards the statue.

After I had read the plaque beneath it, I sighed in the same way one does upon seeing an act of deception taking place before one's eyes. I tried controlling my anger but could not. I gave the statue a kick, but it damaged only the plaster and couldn't break the entire statue. So I picked up a huge piece of rock and hurled it at its head. Half the statue was demolished and the debris of plaster fell on the plinth. I once again read the name written on the plaque: my name—preceded by the word *shaheed.*

The government had taken advantage of my absence of four years, listed me as an S.P.O. and declared me as having been killed by the Naxalites. They had also perhaps embezzled the compensation money that was due to my family or dependants. Whatever the case, I wasn't going to accept a statue built for me while I was still alive.

That entire scene got me thinking. How could the government declare me dead when they knew that I was alive? How could they recruit me as an S.P.O. when I wasn't in the village at all? Which dead body did they strip of its identity to give it my name? Who benefited from it? My father was dead. My sister had left the house. The only person left in my family who could claim compensation was my mother, who could hardly be bothered whether I lived or died. But yes, I knew that my mother could go to any length for money. She was as greedy as she was wicked. While leaving the village four years ago, I had heard whispers that my mother supplied young girls from the village to the policemen. I was aware that in villages like mine, it wasn't an easy task to have the compensation amount approved by the government. One had to run from pillar to post, bribing all and sundry. Did my mother really bribe someone to have me declared a martyr? If yes, then in which form was that bribe paid?

I was dizzy, unable to think, yet forcing myself to think of all that had happened or was happening. It's possible that the number of those who had died at the hands of the Naxalites had been inflated, and I was just a number. But what was the purpose of this lie? I couldn't think of an answer, but I did understand how important dead bodies were to a government.

I looked up at the row of martyrs. Then I kicked at the rubble of my statue, turned towards the forest, and walked on. The sun was setting. I had left the statues far behind. I felt relieved to have come so far away from them, like I had been exorcised of some evil spirit. But my relief wasn't going to last for long.

In the middle of the forest, I reached a deserted village and its burnt houses. Beside those houses, there was a row of graves. At each grave, there was tucked a crudely forged iron figurine of the sickle-hammer insignia and a red flag bearing the same insignia. The redness of most of the flags had faded.

I stopped again, for the names of those *martyrs* too were written on their graves, and I felt compelled to read them. The first grave was Soyam Rukni's. Rukni was the daughter of Soyam Ganga and the sister of Soyam Narwa, who had been declared a martyr by the government. The next grave belonged to Madavi Sannu, who was the second son of my uncle Madavi Ayit and the younger brother of Madavi Budraiya, who had been declared a martyr by the government. The third grave was Sodi Sukram's, the son of Sodi Budhra's younger brother and the cousin of Sodi Adama. Sodi Adama's family and mine did not get along well.

Reading the names on the rest of the graves was unnecessary, for the picture was clear. The villagers had been segregated into two parts, both parts being controlled by powerful, opposing forces. There were an equal number of villagers in both parts. Several men were enrolled as Special Police Officers and an equal number were recruited as Maoist cadets. Villagers on both sides died in equal numbers, either in a crossfire or a landmine explosion.

It was late afternoon. The sun's pale yellow rays fell on the sickle-hammer figurines and their shadows fell on the graves in a row, as if connecting them all.

The material from this complicated war would serve the purpose of sociologists and historians in the future. Research studies would be conducted on the concrete statues of Special Police Officers and the humble graves of Maoists. A number of theses and books would be written on them. But this land, this earth, this part of the world where this complicated war was being fought, would perhaps be forgotten.

I took one last look at that abandoned village and then continued on my way. The evening shadows had begun to fall and the forest was getting denser. Finally, there came a point where the path ended.

The sun had set by now. There were a few stars in the sky. I walked blindly, without any sense of direction, for two hours, until I reached a tree in a clearing. A huge banyan tree, with branches broad enough to allow a man to sleep on them. I knew this place. I knew this banyan tree. It was the same tree from that terrifying night when I was ten years old.

I don't know why, just being under that tree made me feel protected. I decided to spend the night there. I placed my backpack under the tree and sat down. For some time, I was surrounded by the noise of crickets and the blinking of fireflies. Then, a stillness dawned, and in the stillness, I felt as if I had come closer to Silence. Silence. My sister. I couldn't help but remember those times when my sister and I were together. The memories were like wounds, wounds I had thought would heal during my time in college and on the ship. They hadn't. Silence had begun rubbing those wounds and there was no passion I could use to keep silence in check. Silence was always more powerful than passion. Passion could be controlled, but it was difficult to even capture silence.

CHAPTER 8

# Forest

I was a student of standard nine when I saw silence completely take over my sister. I wasn't aware at the time of the people my sister was involved with, but I was observant enough to sense the changes in her and realise that things were not as before. My school was far away from the village, so I couldn't track the people my sister met while I was away; but after I returned home from school, I made sure to keep an eye on her.

Kako, on her part, had become very secretive. Earlier, she'd get me ready for school and drop me halfway, after which she went into the forest to gather leaves and other forest produce. Later, though, I saw her getting up very early in the morning, when it was still dark, tiptoe out of the house, and go into the forest with a basket. Earlier, she would keep the basket in which she collected the forest produce in the yard or outside the house. She did not keep it covered with leaves or grass. Later, she started bringing her basket inside the house, nicely covered with leaves and dried grass, and hid it in the attic behind the house where we kept firewood and cowdung cakes that we burnt as fuel in the chulha.

I got up suddenly one night and saw her hunched before a lit hurricane lamp, her baskets lying near her, intently making some calculations. She was touching, again and again, the ridges of her fingers with her thumb, memorising the figures, peering into the baskets, then again counting on her fingers. Earlier, she used to make me calculate the money she spent at the market. Now, she had learnt to make calculations on her own. She also mumbled something as she counted, but I could not hear her clearly. After observing her for some time, I understood that she was counting some bundles and packets that lay in the baskets. However, I could not understand what kind of bundles and packets a mere Adivasi girl, who collected leaves and fruits from the forest, was counting in the middle of the night. What was so urgent about these calculations that they had to be made in the middle of the night?

After she had finished counting, she put out the lamp. Some time passed in the darkness. Then, there was a rustling behind the house, near the well where she had given me a bath to wash the Other off my being. Then—three times. The flashlight shone three times. One, two, three. In quick succession. Through a gap in the door that opened towards the back, towards the well.

Pin-drop silence.

I shut my eyes tight. Forced my body to freeze.

I heard the door being unlatched and the creaking as it opened. My sister stood at the door like an otherworldly being in the moonlight. She extended her hands outside the door.

I saw her turning around, a basket in her hand. The way she was holding it suggested that it was quite heavy. She set the basket down on the ground, near the other baskets with the packets and bundles she had been counting a while back.

She went to the door again and returned with a second basket.

Then again, third basket.

Then again, fourth basket.

After she had placed the fourth basket on the ground, she picked up the very first one with the bundles and packets and took it to the door. A figure appeared at the door, removed the leaves covering the contents of the basket and counted the bundles and packets. Then there was a conversation between that figure and my sister. Very brief, almost in whispers. Then the figure left with the basket and my sister latched the door from the inside.

My heart was racing. I didn't know what the exchange was about, but I could sense that it was something dangerous.

After that I fell asleep, but woke up again hearing a noise at the door. This time, it was the front door, not the back one. My sister opened the door, picked up one of the baskets, and, shutting the door behind her, tiptoed out of the house in the darkness.

I got up immediately, searched for a matchbox and lit the hurricane lamp. Removing the leaves covering the remaining three baskets that my sister had left behind, I peered inside. I wasn't nervous anymore. I was prepared to accept whatever I was about to see.

The first basket was filled with live bullets. The second basket had detonator wires, boxes of gunpowder and medicines. The third basket had about a dozen revolvers, five or six hand grenades and four bundles of printed pamphlets. I covered all the baskets again with leaves, the way my sister had done.

I heard some rustling outside the house, so I put off the hurricane lamp and kept it aside. Then I returned to bed and pretended to sleep. Kako opened the door and entered. She had two girls with her. They were about the same age as my sister. Each one picked up a basket and tiptoed out of the house.

I couldn't focus at school the next day. My mind was fixed on my sister and her secret activities. What was the meaning of it all? And what would be the consequences?

After dinner that night, I sat in the glow of the hurricane lamp, my schoolbooks open before me. But my mind was elsewhere. Kako finished all the housework for the day and entered our room, wiping her wet hands on her clothes. She came near me and sat with her back against the wall. I too closed my books and sat with my back against the wall. We sat like that, without speaking to each other, for a long time. Knowing that something was wrong with me or that something was worrying me came easily to my sister. I knew that she knew that I knew.

She turned her head towards me, but I did not look at her. I sat glum, silent. Kako touched my hand, but I kept looking at the flame inside the chimney of the hurricane lamp. Kako came closer and touched her face to mine. I still did not move. She grabbed my face with her hands and turned it towards her.

That was the first time in my life that I looked into my sister's eyes. Before that day, anything like that would have been unthinkable. Perhaps she herself wanted me to look into her eyes. She too was looking at me as if she were seeing me for the first time.

I don't know what she saw in me, but I wasn't able to see anything in her. After holding my face for some time, she caressed my head and leaned it on her shoulder.

I couldn't read her eyes, but I could feel that she had forced herself to make me try to read her eyes. That night, I couldn't sense love in my sister's touch. Instead, there was an urgency, an eagerness to come to a release, a catharsis. It was a difficult night. I felt as if everything between my sister and me had been demolished.

Had we only talked, we could have cleared up at least some doubts. But we didn't. Perhaps, she did try to ask me with her eyes if I was all right, if there was something on my mind. Perhaps I couldn't read the question. Perhaps I did not understand my sister.

I moved my head away from her shoulder. She was still looking at me. I thought there was another question in her eyes. I thought she was asking me if I trusted her, or did I think what she was doing was wrong.

The hurricane lamp went out just then and I couldn't see my sister's eyes anymore. Both of us retired to our beds.

Around midnight, once again, a flashlight shone three times at our backdoor. This time, neither of us was asleep. Before getting up, she looked at me, and I looked back at her.

In the darkness, it wasn't possible to read each other's eyes. She squeezed my hand lightly, then stood up and opened the door.

Seven shadows entered through the door into our room. My sister shut the door once they were all inside. She lit a smaller oil lamp this time. I saw that there was no objection in her eyes; she saw that there was no consternation in mine.

What came after that though, I wasn't quite prepared for. But I had understood by then that my house had turned into a stage for an event that would certainly have consequences.

The seven shadows that had entered the room my sister and I shared were seven young girls. They must have been just a few years older than me. They were all dressed in guerrilla fatigues and each one held a gun. As soon as the lamp was lit, quickly, without any hesitation, they took off all their clothes, even their underwear. And as quickly as they had undressed, my sister dressed those seven girls in the traditional attire of the women of the Bhatra community: a plain cotton sari, and ornaments in the ears and nose, and around the neck, arms and legs. Not only that, she dressed their short hair in the traditional hairdo of the Bhatra women, complete with a small comb stuck in the chignon. And if that were not enough, she tattooed traditional patterns on their wrists and upper arms. All of that happened so fast that I could only gape in astonishment.

Once the seven girls were ready, my sister brought seven baskets from the attic where we kept firewood and cowdung cakes. The girls folded the butts of their guns in unison. Then they put the guns, uniforms and boots in seven different baskets—one basket for each girl—and covered them with tendu leaves.

Then they all sat down, my sister and those seven girls, and began talking. In whispers. Their conversation ended when, all of a sudden, in the middle of the night, a rooster crowed somewhere outside the house. One of the girls nodded her head in a decisive way and my sister stood up and opened the door. She looked this side and that. Then she signalled to the seven girls, who stood up and, in single file, walked out of the house. No one could tell they weren't women from the Bhatra community.

My sister bade farewell to the soldiers of the night, shut the door and came and lay down beside me. We lay in silence for a long time. There was so much we could have said, so much we could have talked about, so many questions we could have asked, so many questions we could have answered. But nothing. The entire night passed in silence; not one word came out of our mouths. We lay frozen, neither turning towards nor moving away from one another. As if silence had taken hold of not just my sister but the both of us.

Tonight was similar; as puzzling, secretive and tense. I was again in the forest, not on some childish whim but out of a strong, mature determination.

I was again beneath that same banyan tree, the stem and each branch of which was deeply etched in my memory, sitting upon which I saw one night, all those years ago, Death defeating a struggle for survival. This tree changed my life. It taught me how to remain unmoved by things happening around me and live life as emotionlessly as an animal. This banyan tree was to me worth more than the Bodhi tree.

I took a sheet out of my backpack and spread it on the ground under the banyan tree. I lay down on the sheet expecting to fall asleep soon. I couldn't. I was assailed by thoughts and questions. *Why had I come into the forest? Had I come to look for my sister or to know the reasons that had separated her from me? Even if I found her, would I be able to take her away from what had separated us?* My sister's leaving home and joining the Dada Log in the forest was no secret. It was known to all that, in the past few years, my sister had reached the top rank among the Maoists. *Was there any reason she'd be willing to return with me?* This personal search operation of mine would be futile if I failed to change the circumstances that had separated me from my sister. But was I in a position to change those circumstances? I was just an outsider here, in the forest. Even my objectives were not clear. What was I seeking? Where would I look?

I looked at the moon through the banyan's branches and closed my eyes, expecting sleep, expecting peace, even if for a short while. But how could a person find peace while being part of a community ravaged by violence? How could I expect to sleep peacefully in the midst of all this violence? When I was a child, I witnessed an act of violence taking place here, beneath this banyan tree, and yet I was able to fall into a deep slumber. But I wasn't a child anymore, and violence had moved away from the shade of this tree to all over. The violence I saw all those years ago had a reason: hunger. The animals were hungry and had no means other than violence to assuage their hunger. Today, those animals had been replaced by humans.

But what did they hunger for? And didn't they have any means other than violence to douse it?

Fog surrounded the forest as the night progressed. The cold wind blowing from Kanger Valley and the hills of Bailadila touched me. I took out one more sheet from my bag and covered myself with it. The fog deepened. The noise of crickets gained pitch.

About half an hour later, I heard the call of a bird. It was an anxious call, as if the bird had sensed a predator approaching. But a bird calling at that time of the night? How big was the predator?

Just moments later, I heard footsteps in the fog. I got up quickly, packed my sheets in the bag, and climbed up the tree. I took up position on the same branch where I had spent a fearful night years ago.

The sounds came closer. In a short while, I saw a row of humans gather under the tree. There must have been ten or twelve people in the group. They stood facing the tree with their heads lowered. They were dressed like villagers. They looked terrified. It was evident that they had been forced to gather under the tree.

Some moments later, seven or eight gunmen emerged from the fog. They were dressed in the uniform of the paramilitary force and I could tell from what I could see of their faces that they were from the Northeast.

There was, all of a sudden, a blinding flash behind the gunmen. It came from the headlights of a vehicle. I saw in that light, four people: two men and two women. All four wore guerrilla fatigues, the kind that my sister had helped those seven girls change out of one night. Held captive by the gunmen in paramilitary uniforms, they were now made to hold each other's hands. One gunman stood behind each of them, pointing his gun at the captive's head. An order was given, and the gunmen fired. The killing was sudden, yet neat, as if performed after many rehearsals.

Next, the twelve or so villagers were asked to undress. Several of them had only one piece of clothing—a gamchha or a lungi—on their bodies. They placed their clothes in a pile and stood in the glow of the vehicle's headlights, covering their genitals with their hands.

One of the paramilitary gunmen threw a bundle of clothes before the naked villagers. They were guerrilla outfits, the kind of clothes worn by the four people who had just been shot in the head. The naked villagers were ordered to wear the guerrilla outfits.

The villagers were not used to such clothes. Many of them did not even know how to hold them in the right way. Yet, they started putting them on, moving their hands and legs in their own odd way, like a drowning man throws his hands around, trying to stay afloat. The villagers who had been given clothes that did not fit them or those who were unable to fasten the buttons or draw the zippers were sweating profusely, not from the effort but because it seemed to them that not being able to get into these clothes was a crime worth being punished for.

Once dressed up, the villagers were made to stand in a row. An order was given and bullets were fired. To dress up the killing as an encounter, the bodies were picked up and thrown in different directions.

The paramilitary gunmen dusted their uniforms and got into the vehicle. Once they had all boarded, the vehicle began moving along the same route by which I had come. Gradually, it began to recede into the fog and only its glowing, red tail lights were faintly visible.

*BOOM!*

A ball of fire shot up in the air and the forest lit up.

Before the red tail lights of the paramilitary vehicle could disappear into the fog, an explosion destroyed it and all the men on board. When the fire and the smoke cleared, I saw body parts of the dead paramilitary splattered everywhere.

After a minute or so, when it was confirmed that none of the paramilitary gunmen had survived, forty to fifty Maoists emerged from the bushes, picked up the weapons and bullets belonging to the dead men and retreated into the bushes as quickly and stealthily as they had appeared.

I clung to the branch of the banyan tree. My heart was throbbing and I was unsure if I'd be able to hold on much longer. Yet, in some time, a great tiredness overcame me; I yawned and fell asleep. I was woken up in the morning by the chirping of a bird on the tree.

The forest was still wrapped in fog. Perched on the branch on which I had slept, the bird twittered loudly. When I stirred, she flew away. Then, after flying around in a circle, she came and sat on the same branch and began twittering again. Was she trying to tell me something? I understood soon enough. She was perhaps asking me not to move, for very close to my right hand, on the branch next to mine, lay her nest. I peered over and saw two chicks. So small, so untouched by anything in the world outside their nest. For some time, I kept looking at the life that had been born on the tree that I had come to associate only with death.

The curtain had fallen on a cruel act that had played out under this tree the night before. Bodies were strewn everywhere. Of the Maoists, the villagers, and the paramilitary. But this cruel act was performed by humans. The trees and animals and birds were unconcerned with it all and had set out on their daily routine. I too got down carefully from the banyan tree and set off.

After walking some distance in the forest, I stopped beside a Salfi tree—the jaggery palm tree—from which the juice was dripping. I fashioned a bowl out of a leaf, collected the sap and drank to my fill. It was my first meal after entering the forest.

I came out of the forest and reached a dirt track. I began walking on it, not knowing where it would lead me. I heard the sound of an automobile behind me. Turning around, I saw a jeep approaching, negotiating the curves on the unpaved forest path. It was a ramshackle jeep, out of repair, and it was carrying more people than its capacity. There were people stuffed inside it; there were people standing on the carrier at the top; there were people standing on the footboards on the sides and the rear, hanging from the carrier. They all looked anxious, as if they were escaping from somewhere.

I guessed right, for that jeep was followed by more jeeps, all of them similarly overcrowded. The news of the landmine blast from the previous night had spread like wildfire and the villagers were running away from their homes, expecting a retaliatory combing operation by the paramilitary forces. I looked closely and saw that there were people not only inside the vehicles but also in the bushes by the dirt track. I hadn't noticed them earlier, but they were visible to me now. All of them looked fearful. All of them were escaping, and they were too scared to walk openly on the road.

When the vehicles had passed and I resumed walking on the road, I felt as if somebody had joined me, somebody had begun walking behind me. I turned around to look at him. He was a middle-aged man, clothed only in a lungi, and he held a spear in his hand.

Upon seeing the man walking behind me, several people came out of the bushes and began to follow me and him. I turned around and saw hundreds of men and women following me. They were all my own people. They all held bows and arrows and axes and hatchets in their hands. Perhaps they felt safe in a group. They weren't talking to one another; they were just looking at me and following me, adjusting their pace to mine. As if they'd chosen me to lead their group. As if walking behind me was a strategy for survival. Unknowingly, whether I liked it or not, I had become a leader.

We walked for nearly fifteen-twenty minutes. Several times, I slowed down and gave them the opportunity to overtake me and move ahead. But they didn't. They just kept adjusting their pace to mine and continued following me. I was obliged to lead this group of anxious people.

At a bend in the road, we encountered the vehicles that had preceded us. They stood to the left of the road. The ramshackle jeep stood at the front. I went closer and saw why they were unable to move ahead.

Just in front of the ramshackle jeep, there were two huge trees that had been felled. A few feet beyond the trees, the path had been dug deep. And beyond that trench stood a battalion of paramilitary forces. Two anti-landmine vehicles of the Naga Battalion and two army trucks were also positioned there.

It was clear that this was a fallout of the explosion from the previous night.

However, the situation was somewhat even, for the escaping villagers and the paramilitary forces were both faced with the same difficulty. How to move ahead with a trench dug in the road and two felled trees beyond it?

The commander of the Naga Battalion had eyes like those of a cat, sharp and piercing. He sized me up, taking me to be the leader of the escaping villagers. By that time, sixteen commandos had alighted from the anti-landmine vehicles and taken their position on the other side of the trench. Among the men and women who had followed me, furious whispers had begun in Halbi and Hindi, so furious that they sounded like the susurration a flame makes on the wick before detonating a clump of gunpowder. The villagers tightened their grip on their axes and hatchets, preparing to fight.

My hand automatically went inside my pocket where I sought guidance from Passion. The commander immediately aimed his pistol at me. I wasn't perturbed though. For I wasn't like these villagers. I wasn't a part of the escaping crowd. They might consider me their leader, but I wasn't their leader. The paramilitary forces might think that I was leading a band of rebels, but I wasn't. I was going on my own journey. I had nothing to do with either the Maoists or the paramilitary or even the villagers.

But how could I convey this to the people aiming their guns at me and to those who had followed me? Avoiding a bloodbath was possibly what we all sought at that juncture.

Finding no way out of the deadlock, I clenched Passion tightly in my fist, pulled my hand out of my pocket, and held it out for the commander to see. I raised my eyebrows, as if smiling at him, asking him: *This is what I've got. Are you going to do something about it?* The commander saw that what I held in my hand was a mere stone. The sternness on his face dissolved into a smirk and he returned his pistol to the holster at his waist. Behind me, the whispering stopped.

I turned around to face the villagers and shook my head. Their grips on their weapons loosened. On the other side of the trench, the commander signalled to his commandos and they got down from the vans to move the trees aside. When I looked at the villagers again, they stepped forward and began hacking the fallen trees with their hatchets. In some time, the felled trees had been moved out of the path and the trench had been adequately filled so as to allow the passage of vehicles. When the vehicles began to move, leaving a big cloud of dust in their wake, I separated myself from the group that had followed me, veered away from the path, and began walking down a slope in the direction of South Bastar.

After going some distance, I looked back up at the road. The commander too had stepped off the path and was looking at me.

I climbed back up and stood before him. Our eyes locked for a few moments before, all of a sudden, he flung his pistol at me. It was sudden, but I was alert enough. I caught the pistol, and as swiftly as he had thrown it at me, I flung the pistol back at him. He too caught it expertly. Then he smiled at me. I understood that he was a seasoned soldier, one who could keep his calm and sense of humour even in tense moments. I understood how dangerous men like him could be.

Then he did something quite unexpected. He took from the holster around his waist two grenades, making me worry whether he would throw them at me and whether I would have to catch them. But he didn't. He started juggling the grenades, throwing them up and then catching them. And, all the while, his eyes, I saw, were not on the grenades—his gaze was fixed on me.

When his juggling ended, I acknowledged it with a smile, feeling quite broken on the inside upon realising that this acrobatic feat, as well as the martial arts, of the Adivasis of Nagaland never did them any good. Their talent and traditions had become mere exhibits. The real acrobatics are done in the capital of the country. The people at the centre of power do not consider the people from Northeastern India as anything more than mere chattels. Sometimes they are sent to guard the borders of the country and, sometimes, to the interiors of the country to crush people's movements started by other Adivasis like them, all in the name of internal security.

I shook myself out of that thought. Every person had the right to choose their own means of livelihood, whether they ploughed fields or shot guns. I was no one to judge which path they chose to make ends meet. Circumstances can force a farmer to pick up a gun. Similar circumstances may cause a person shooting guns to turn to farming. Unless I had walked in their shoes, I was no one to judge the choices they made. I was no one to imagine what the consequences of their choice would be.

I saw the commander return the grenade to its holster and turn around and leave. I too turned towards the slope and began walking down. It took me a full two hours to come down the hill, at the foot of which was a narrow track. There were no markers on that track—no signboard, no milestone. It was impossible to tell where I was and which places it connected.

I remembered that I had started my journey in the east. I began walking towards what I presumed was the south. After some time, I came across two road rollers and two asphalt pavers—all of them burnt and damaged. At a little distance were two discharge loaders, both burnt. I could guess that there had been a tussle between those who wanted to build roads and those who didn't want the roads to be built. Those who had wanted to build roads had been successful for a kilometre or two—after that, they had escaped with their lives.

A crow sat on one of the burnt discharge loaders, cawing loudly. I wondered why it was cawing at this point suspended between development and desolation. Perhaps it was wondering why so many people were coming into the forest, some with equipment to build roads, others with equipment to break roads that had been built. Perhaps it also wondered where the people in between those two extremes had gone. Where was that man wearing only a loincloth, holding an axe or a bow in one hand and a rooster or a gourd canteen filled with mahua wine in the other? Where was that woman with a bundle of tendu leaves on her head or a child in her arms? Perhaps the crow was cawing because it couldn't see anymore the sights it was so used to seeing.

It was afternoon. I ate whatever I found on the way. I dug up edible roots from the ground and plucked Manila tamarind fruits and half-ripe guavas from the trees. I ate some and also dropped some into my bag to eat later. After travelling some distance, I found a clear stream, took off my clothes, and dipped my body in the cool water. I closed my eyes as I lay in the stream. Lying like that for a long time, I mumbled quite spontaneously, 'You're the best river in the world. I am very grateful to you.' I don't know why I was reminded of the way my sister bathed me when I was a child, pouring bucket upon bucket of cool water over my body.

The stream flowed down a rocky slope. On its bank, I discovered a small cove, large enough for me to curl up in. I decided to spend the night there. Clearing the cove of stones, I spread my sheet on the ground. By quarter to seven, it was dark everywhere. So dark, I could see stars in the clear sky. In the silence of the jungle, the sound of the gurgling stream lulled me to sleep.

I woke up the next morning to a cool breeze blowing on my face. I remembered to thank the stream and the cove before moving on. I walked down the rocky slope to a point where the stream widened enough to resemble a small river. I understood that I had reached the foot of the hill. I crossed the river at a spot where the water was shallow. Then I walked away from it. I had nothing else to say to it, not even another word of gratitude. My mind had gone blank.

I ate the fruits I had collected the previous day. I was ready to go on another hike. It was already noon when I reached a road which was, to my surprise, paved with asphalt. I saw a milestone too by the road. Etched on it was the name of a village, Errabor, five kilometres away. I reached Errabor in about an hour.

There was a relief camp in Errabor. I decided to try my luck and look for my mother there. I walked up to the check post of the camp and told the two policemen who were posted there my name, my mother's name and the name of my village. They looked at each another and their faces broke into sly, knowing smiles. A third policeman came up with a wireless set in his hand. He asked me my name and my purpose for being here at the relief camp. I repeated my name and other details to the third policeman who relayed the information via the wireless set. Upon receiving permission from the other side, he ordered the smiling policemen to lift the barrier for me. I entered. The third policeman informed me that the number of my mother's cabin was 168 and it was in the eleventh lane.

There were several cabins on both sides of the road I was walking on. People peered at me from these cabins. I reached the place where the ration was distributed. There was a booth with a window in the middle of the path. Policemen inside the booth distributed rations through the window. There was a huge crowd outside the booth and, instead of standing in a queue, people had crowded around the window. They were all shouting in Gondi. From what I could understand, they were agitated because they had not been given rations for the last three days. The Special Police Officers there were shouting back at the people in Gondi, 'If you give your ration to the Dada Log, you won't be given ration anymore.' The people shouted back, 'No, it's a lie. We don't give our ration to anyone. If the government cannot give us rations, then let the government shoot and kill us instead of keeping us hungry.'

I reached the eleventh lane. A collective lament of hunger from the women and children in the cabins there greeted me. Was I in a relief camp or a torture camp?

Cabin No. 168 was closed and no sound came from within. That startled me. All the cabins I had walked past so far were open. I saw people crying in hunger or resignedly staring outside. The silence of the inmates seemed to shriek. Then how come my mother's cabin was shut? Was she asleep? Was she unwell?

I dropped my backpack at the door and knocked. There was no response from inside. I waited awhile and knocked again, louder.

'Who is it?'

It was Yaya's voice. I was hearing my mother's voice after four years, but I felt no joy on hearing it.

'It's me,' I said and tried to imagine what my mother's response upon seeing me would be.

Yaya opened the door a crack, just enough for her eyes to be able to peer outside.

'Why have you come here?' she hissed. In her eyes, I saw neither sorrow nor anger, only disgust.

'I want to come in,' I said, pushing the door. 'Open the door.'

'This isn't your father's house!' she shouted at me. 'Get lost!'

I was so stunned and angry at my mother's outburst that I stopped pushing the door; I just gave it one tight kick. It flew open and my mother was thrown somewhere inside.

What I saw inside the cabin explained why she had tried to prevent me from entering and why the policemen at the check post had smiled knowingly when I asked them about her.

There were two military sleeping kits spread on the ground. On one sat a man from the Naga Battalion, his back propped against the wall, his legs spread, his pants at his knees. In one hand he held a machine gun; in the other the head of an underage Adivasi girl. The girl's head was bent over the man's crotch and his penis was inside her mouth. On the other sleeping kit, I saw the naked buttocks of another man thrusting into another underage girl who lay naked, pressed under his body. While the first man pointed his gun at me, the second one carried on with his business. The first man signalled something to my mother with his eyes. She signalled back. He then placed his gun on the ground.

I searched Yaya's face and found not a jot of shame on it. She stood with her arms akimbo, proudly, determinedly.

'Where is Kako?' I asked, looking her in the eye.

'How would I know? You're the one who should know.'

'Me?'

'Yes, you. You slept with her. You two fondled and kissed each other all night. And now you're asking me?'

Given how obscene her words and manner of speaking were, it was a miracle I didn't explode. I cannot say how I restrained myself.

'Look, give me straight answers,' I told her. 'I'm not here to waste my time with you.'

'Straight answers? Are you even bothered about who lives and who dies that you're demanding straight answers from me?'

'What do you mean, who lives and who dies?'

'Your sister's friends killed your father,' she nearly spat at my face, staring at me in disgust.

For a moment, I wasn't in a position to say anything. I felt dizzy. It felt like I would collapse.

'What?' I managed to mumble.

'Why are you asking me?' She was ready with her answers. 'Go and ask that bitch who is sleeping with her friends in the forest.'

'I am asking *you*,' I said but I felt weak. 'Tell me what happened.'

'Who are you to ask questions?' Yaya started screaming at the top of her lungs. 'Asking questions, huh! Where were you when that sister of yours left home and went away? Where were you when the police picked up your father because of your sister's adventures? Where were you when your sister's friends slit your father's throat for spying for the police? And now you come here asking questions?'

It was useless. My standing there was useless. My asking questions was useless. Which questions should I ask? And who should I ask? Not only my mother, every inmate, every survivor in that relief camp had suffered devastation. So who could I go to? Should I question that period in time? That period in time when humans were reduced to mere pawns in a huge game. That period in time when humans were being torn apart, crushed. That period in time when violence, counter-violence, rape and carnage became normal. Everything that was happening in the villages, in the forest, in the camp, in this cabin was *normal*.

The girl who had been raped in front of me now sat with her knees folded against her body, looking at me so normally, as if what had just happened was routine. These girls did not show any pain, any indignation, any rage. They reminded me of that elephant, the one that had been tied to a banyan tree, the one that had accepted its fate and surrendered to the ravenous wild dogs. For me, the sight inside my mother's cabin was revolting, but for those who had accepted their fate, it was just normal.

When I came out of the cabin, the camp was in an uproar. The inmates—men, women and children—who had gathered in front of the ration booth were running helter-skelter, screaming, shouting out to one another. The Special Police Officers and the goons of the Salwa Judum were chasing them, hitting them with sticks and batons. The Salwa Judum was, apparently, a counter-insurgency operation that had been launched in Bastar. Its name was taken from the Gondi language and meant 'purification drive'. But the Salwa Judum, the operation, was far from purifying. From what I knew and understood, it should have been named 'oppression drive'.

A crowd ran screaming past my mother's cabin, and I went back in, instead of leaving. The beatings and uproar outside had no impact here. Having finished their business, the two men had stood up and were wearing their pants. My mother had started clearing away chicken bones, cigarette stubs and alcohol bottles. It was unbearable for me to even look at what she was doing. I came out of the cabin again and walked away.

The camp had quietened down. The goons of the Salwa Judum were returning after chasing the inmates into their cabins. Children still peered hungrily outside their cabins even as their mothers pulled them back inside.

A van with grilles affixed to its windows stopped at the ration booth. When the inmates saw the van, they left their cabins and began running away. Those who ran were beaten with sticks. Those who fell to the ground and injured themselves were stuffed into the vehicle. The van rounded up several people and left, leaving smoke, dust and a deathly silence in its wake.

For two months after that, I kept roaming from one relief camp to the other, even though what I saw at the camp in Errabor was more than what I could accept. I was unmindful of what I ate, what I drank, how I sustained myself. I had stopped thinking about myself altogether. I just looked at how an entire community had been uprooted from their land and, under the guise of being protected by the police, was being prepared for the onslaught of a bigger power; and how all of it was being perceived as something *normal*.

The number of refugees was increasing by the day. Every village, big and small, was being forcefully vacated and the villagers were being stuffed into camps. Witnessing the displacement, the hordes of refugees—it was maddening. I walked with the refugees to the camps they were allotted. I had become one of them. For two whole months, I was unable to think straight. I had nearly forgotten the purpose of my return, forgotten why I had gone into the forest, what I had sought to find there.

At one of the camps, I was afflicted by an infection of the bowels. I became dehydrated and nearly unconscious. I don't remember who picked me up from that camp and took me deep into the forest. There were such tall trees there that sunlight hardly reached the ground; it seemed like evening even during daytime. There were no cabins in the forest. Plastic sheets were spread on the ground and roofs were created by tying plastic sheets to trees. The people who had taken me there had their own blankets, utensils to cook their meals in, and every person had their own bag and a gun.

I was kept in that place for two days. My captors brought a doctor from a relief camp to treat me. No one asked me even once how I was feeling. They just pointed a gun at the doctor, as if he wouldn't be spared if anything untoward happened to me. The doctor felt my pulse, placed the bell of his stethoscope on my chest, and gave me injections. But even after twenty-four hours, my condition remained the same. The cramps in my abdomen wouldn't subside, and I just went on shitting watery and smelly stool. The plastic sheet on which I had been made to lie down was completely smeared with my shit. My captors kept changing the sheets every few hours.

'His stools won't stop unless he is given I.V. fluids,' the doctor said to one of my captors who wasn't holding a gun. He seemed like a senior cadre of the platoon.

'Don't you have any other way?' he asked the doctor.

'Please do this for me,' the doctor said, holding out a key in his hand. 'Go to my camp. My cabin is in the fourth lane. There is an almirah in my cabin. You'll find I.V. fluids and some injections inside it. Please bring all of it. But be very careful. I have been with you all for two days now. If anyone comes to know ...'

The captor placed a reassuring hand on the doctor's shoulder. Then he called two members of his platoon to one side and explained something to them. The men nodded their heads. They changed from their guerrilla fatigues into plain clothes, and, leaving their guns behind, left for the relief camp. They returned with the supplies after nearly two hours, running and panting. I wondered why they were putting all this effort into healing me.

I was immediately put on I.V. fluids. The doctor injected three vials of some medicine into the I.V. bottle at a gap of fifteen minutes. I began sweating. Then, after a while, I was able to breathe evenly, and soon fell into a deep sleep.

When I woke up the next morning, I was being carried away somewhere. The two men carrying me did so deftly, as if they were used to doing this work. The other members of the platoon were walking with us, their plastic sheets, utensils and kits on their backs and guns on their shoulders. I was feeling better. My mind was clear and stable. I could hear the men talking and understood what they said.

I heard them mention my sister's name every now and then, with a lot of respect. I understood that they were my sister's friends and that I was, at this time, in a guerrilla zone.

We reached a shady spot inside the forest after walking for nearly four hours. A clearing had been made after cutting down a few trees. My sister's friends first spread a plastic sheet on the ground and made me lie down on it. After that, they started unloading their belongings. Once they had placed everything on the ground, they sat down for some time to rest. I saw the two men who had carried me here. One of them was quite young, just a boy, and did not seem as tired as his companions. I looked at him with gratitude. He smiled back at me. Later, they wrapped me in a plastic sheet to guard me against the dew that would fall at night.

After resting for some time, two people left with buckets to fetch water, while two others began gathering dried wood and branches. They lit a makeshift chulha and began boiling water and tea leaves in an aluminium vessel. By that time, another man had mixed milk powder with water, which was poured into the boiling tea. Once the tea was ready, it was sieved into plastic cups and served around.

There was so much calm here, it was unnerving. The routine manner in which my sister's friends were performing the various tasks—cooking, bringing water, cleaning up—gave the impression that they were running a household. All of which completely belied the fact that we were, at the time, on a battlefield and that those people were actually rebels who had waged a war against the system. How easily they had become used to life inside the forest! How well they had adjusted and calibrated their lives to the tough situations in the forest. Even after spending two months in the forest and the various relief camps, I was finding this sort of existence difficult. How difficult it must have been for these guerrilla cadets when they left everything to join this mission. Did they even remember that they were once a part of the large civilisation outside the forest? Did they remember their families and loved ones? Were they aware of the fact that no matter how far they walked and how many locations they changed or how stealthily they fought, one day they would have to ...

I held back my thoughts. Who was I to determine their fate? How could I, after spending barely three days with the cadets, imagine what might happen to them?

The senior cadre whom the doctor had convinced to bring I.V. fluids for me brought me a cup of tea. He sat beside me and asked, 'How are you feeling now?'

'Better.' I smiled at him, then added, 'Perhaps I'm one of those unfortunate people who never get to know who their benefactors are.'

The man looked at me with a certain tenderness in his eyes. He patted my shoulder and said, 'Seventeen people in that camp were infected. You are one of the two fortunate people who survived.'

I was stunned. I had no idea that the affliction was so dangerous and had spread so wide.

'Did those fifteen people die because they couldn't find treatment in time?' I asked.

The man did not answer. Then he said, 'Tomorrow, we will put you on a bus that will take you to Jagdalpur. Once you reach Jagdalpur, you're free to go wherever you wish. But you have to leave Bastar within two days.'

I observed a sudden change come upon him.

'Whose order is it that I have to leave Bastar within two days?' I asked him. 'Is it yours or your area commander's?'

He looked up at me and said, 'This isn't an order, my friend. If you acknowledge that we've saved your life, then we demand from you that you leave Bastar within two days.'

I nodded, took a long sip of tea and said, 'I'll leave, but I had come into the forest for a purpose. Perhaps I won't be able to achieve that.'

He stood up and left without saying anything.

The medicines I had been given in the morning were working. No more cramps. I was able to lie down comfortably and stayed that way till afternoon.

The aroma of rice cooking on a wood fire began to spread. After the rice was done, a vessel with dal was placed on the chulha. While the dal was cooking, the members of the platoon sat a little away from me, discussing their plans for the next day.

The young boy who had carried me here had been given the task of chopping vegetables. He sat surrounded by onions, green chillies, tomatoes, cabbage, spinach and potatoes. He sliced all the vegetables with the same speed and almost in the same way. In between, he removed the lid from the vessel on the chulha to check if the dal was cooked. At times, annoyed, he put a ladle into the vessel, took some dal out and tried to mash it with his fingers. He then thrust more wood and dried leaves into the chulha to increase the flame. I could tell that he was hungry and the obstinate dal which was refusing to cook faster was making him angry.

About half an hour later, the meeting of the other platoon members was over. The dal too was ready and a vessel with the chopped vegetables was placed on the chulha. The sound and smell of chillies, onions and ginger splattering in hot oil was so tempting that even I felt hungry despite having been ill for so many days.

The young platoon member could not hold himself back when the food was served on leaf plates and bowls. He hurriedly put a steaming hot morsel into his mouth and immediately winced, shutting his eyes for a long time. The hot morsel made his eyes water and his face flush, but instead of spitting it out, he swallowed it somehow. His impatience amused me and I wondered if he was mature enough to understand the nature of the mission he had joined.

I wasn't served the food though, the food which had been tempered with oil and spices. A female cadet placed another vessel on the chulha and ran a ladle through it. I recalled that she was the same girl who had washed the plastic sheets I had soiled these past three days. I was filled with admiration and gratitude for her.

She was cooking khichadi for me. She ladled it into a leaf bowl and served it to me.

'*Johar.*' She greeted me in the traditional way before handing me the bowl.

The khichadi was delicious. It had moong dal and flax seeds and, just to add some flavour, pieces of crushed peanuts had been sprinkled on it.

'This is very good,' I told the girl.

She said nothing, just smiled shyly.

I had intended to thank her for washing my soiled sheets and for keeping me clean, but I couldn't bring myself to do it.

After having their meal, the cadets opened their bags and took out books and magazines which all of them began reading. They read in silence for two hours. Then they began discussing what they had read. After the discussion, they took out a radio. For fifteen minutes, they listened to the news on the BBC, after which they listened to songs from old Hindi films on the Jaimala show on Vividh Bharati.

When evening fell, I was quite taken aback to see the senior cadre, whom the doctor had requested to have I.V. fluids brought for me, take out a laptop from his bag. What baffled me wasn't that they used a laptop and other modern technology but how they charged a laptop in the middle of a forest. I got my answer soon after, when he took out a solar power charger from his kit.

The laptop and the transistor radio were put on charging mode, and the platoon members began to prepare for the last meal of the day.

While preparations for the meal were on, some cadets were watching videos on YouTube on the laptop. I joined them. Most of the videos were of news shows and current affairs shows. Then they began watching a video in which a woman was arguing quite eruditely. Her voice was clear and she never raised her voice no matter what question or argument was thrown at her. She looked learned, and whatever she said in English was immediately translated into Gondi by the senior cadre and relayed to the other cadets.

When the video ended and the laptop was packed away, I asked the man, 'Who was that lady?'

'She's Arundhati Roy,' he told me. 'We respect her very much.'

I didn't know who Arundhati Roy was, but from the little I saw of her on that video left a deep impact on me.

The evening turned darker and cooler. A soothing breeze began to blow. I still had difficulty believing that I was at a base camp in a guerrilla zone.

The meal at night was as delicious as the one in the afternoon. The girl had prepared two dishes separately for me: cooked jackfruit and a chutney made of coriander, chillies, tomato, ginger and garlic. Just one morsel of each, and I knew whose hand was behind those dishes.

I called the girl close to me and asked, 'From where did you learn to make this chutney and to cook jackfruit in this way?'

She said nothing.

'Did Irma Kako teach you to cook these?'

The girl looked up at me and kept staring, not knowing what to say.

'Irma Kako?' I said. 'Madavi Irma? Did she teach you to cook these?'

The girl lowered her eyes.

I understood that the girl had spent some time with my sister, not only in the war that they were waging but also apart from that, during which she was able to learn from my sister how to cook. Silence was working even here. Silence had extracted me from the camp where I was caught in the jaws of death. Silence had followed me everywhere. Perhaps right from the moment I came out of that police station and decided to walk into the forest.

I couldn't look at the girl anymore. I lowered my eyes to the bowl in my hands and began eating, crying silently as I ate, my tears dropping on the food, on the chutney and the jackfruit dish that were so familiar. I couldn't help my tears from flowing. Perhaps the girl was watching me cry. Perhaps they were all watching me cry. I did not care. I just let my tears flow.

I composed myself when I was done eating. Then I rose to wash my mouth and hand. I ate my medicines and lay down, closing my eyes. Soon, sleep came over me.

What time of the night was it when I woke up? Or did I not wake up at all? Was it just a dream? For my eyes did not open. And I willed them to remain shut.

I heard leaves rustling near my bed. Then I felt someone close to me. I felt fingers combing through my hair and someone caressing my head. Then I smelt the fragrance of jamun. Plump, ripe, purple jamuns.

I felt a kiss on my forehead. I knew it was Silence. I knew Silence had been watching over me all this while. I could have opened my eyes. But I didn't. For I didn't want to.

Silence wasn't the sister I had last seen in my village before I left for Raipur. Silence was a different person now. Would I be able to look at her? Would I be able to accept what she had turned into? The sister I had come looking for in the forest, searching for whom I had watched an entire community being reduced to refugees, their villages burnt and vacated—that sister was Madavi Irma. The sister who sat beside me now, caressing my head, and who—like every time—watched over me, was Silence. Would I be able to see Madavi Irma as Silence?

The fragrance of jamun lingered around me for some time. Then it slowly began shuffling away from me. Away. Away. Then it was lost. That fragrance of jamun was lost, and I sunk again into slumber.

When I got up the next day, I was served tea in bed. I drank the tea, walked around for a while, brushed my teeth, and went into the temporary toilet that had been built a fair distance away from the base camp to relieve myself. When I came out of the toilet, the entire place had been cleared. The plastic sheets, my bed, the cooking utensils—everything had been packed up. It was as if no one had been here yesterday. The platoon members threw dirt over the ash where the makeshift chulha had been built, in order to erase every trace of their night halt at this spot.

The senior cadre came to me with a roll of papers tied tightly with a rubber band. I unrolled the papers to find that they were the documents I had left behind at the police station. The papers which were supposed to have been sent to the headquarters to be inspected. How did they find them? I was filled with respect for the efficiency of these fighters.

I looked with gratitude at the senior cadre, but his face was plain as before, betraying no thought or feeling. I knew that my thanking him would be an unnecessary formality, but I was dying to say something. I had to tell him how much it meant to me, all that they had done for me in the last three days—or perhaps from the time I returned to my village after the stint at sea.

'This work you all are doing ... it's so dangerous ... it takes so much courage and patience.'

He said nothing.

'Why?' I couldn't help but blurt out. 'My rescue? ... These papers? ... Why?'

He looked at me for some time before he said, 'There's no time to talk in detail. As you can see, we are in the midst of a war. Mutual trust and love for one another are what keep us all united. We can take bullets for our comrades. And you are the younger brother of Comrade Madavi Irma. How could we not do this much for you?'

He began walking. The other comrades had already loaded their kits on their backs and their guns on their shoulders.

I wasn't expecting the senior cadre to speak to me anymore, but he did.

'How ironical it is,' he said, 'that you are employed with a shipping company whose cargo is at the root of so much exploitation and so many conflicts!'

I had no answer to that. He was right.

'From here, you will have to go to Vishakhapatnam,' he informed me, 'from where you will sail to Japan. Do you know what you are going to carry this time?'

I shook my head; I hadn't the faintest idea. But I was quite in awe of their network, which had so capably got them so much information.

'The best iron ore from Bastar will be transported by that ship,' he said. 'The best iron ore from Bastar is being sold only for four hundred rupees per tonne!'

'So?' I hesitated a bit before asking.

'So it means that the iron ore is being looted, and we are trying to stop that loot, but you are enabling it by transporting the iron ore.'

'It means that,' I said, 'in some way, I am against your efforts.'

He stopped, smiled and placed his hand on my shoulder. Then he moved his hand and resumed walking.

'This needs to be seen from a broader perspective,' he spoke as he walked. 'If we see you as being against us, then we would need to also see the labourers who are engaged in mining the iron ore as being against us. Similarly, we'd also have to see those labourers as being against us who build roads and railway tracks on which this iron ore is transported. But we are not against the miners and labourers. We never were. Our fight is against the policies made by the government that enable corporate bodies to grab mining leases for free. Our fight is against those agencies which are working on behalf of corporate houses to clear forests and empty out villages.'

The cadre and I spoke for nearly an hour as we walked, and not once did I get the feeling that he was trying to impress me. He did not even ask me if I agreed with him. He tried to answer my questions patiently. It was as if he had an idea in his mind and he was sharing it with me, like one would with a friend.

He stopped at the top of a slope and asked me to go down a track. Then he went ahead, without a word of goodbye, without turning around to check if I had climbed down.

I looked down the slope. A cadet was standing at the base. He was dressed in plain clothes and I wouldn't have been able to tell that he was a cadet if I had not spent three days with him. Taking the track, I climbed down the slope.

I saw a paved road at some distance from where the track ended. Between the road and the track, there was, for a distance of about twenty-five feet, rocky, uneven ground. The cadet held my hand as if he knew that I wouldn't be able to walk on such terrain.

'Why doesn't this track go up to that road?' I asked as I hobbled over the rocks.

'So that those who pass on the road don't come to know that there is a track here.' The comrade smiled at me as he spoke.

'I see!' I said, surprised. How efficiently they covered their tracks!

We were walking on a huge rock when he stopped. There was an abyss, about three feet wide and twenty feet deep. The cadet left my hand and jumped across the abyss. Then he turned towards me and spread his arms, perhaps to hold me in case I lost balance. But I jumped with such a force that I fell over the cadet and we rolled down the rock till the road.

We got up laughing and dusting our clothes.

'Are you hurt?' I began inspecting his body, but he shook his head.

He told me to sit on the rock and we both sat down. We talked. We talked about the leap we had just made. Then he asked me how I had made a leap from the forest to a ship, and I told him my story.

'Wouldn't you want to make a leap from the guerrilla zone to the world outside?' I asked him.

'That will be the last leap,' he laughed. 'It's too early to talk about it now.'

A jeep came and stopped on the road before us. An empty jeep. The cadet and the driver of the jeep spoke with their eyes. The driver signalled to me to get in. I sat in the seat behind the driver's. The cadet touched me on my shoulder. I looked at him and he extended his right hand towards me. I knew he wasn't coming with me. I shook his hand and he squeezed it gently. I remembered Dhananjay. The cadet's hand had the same warmth as Dhananjay's.

After crossing the valley, the driver stepped on the accelerator. There was a village after twelve kilometres or so. The driver stopped the jeep a few feet away from the bus stand in that village and pointed towards a bus. It was a bus to Jagdalpur, and it was ready to leave.

Upon reaching Jagdalpur, I ate at a roadside stall and took a rickshaw straight to the railway station. I had no doubt now, I need not consult Passion, because I knew that it had been decided where I had to go.

I purchased a ticket to Vishakhapatnam and sat on a bench on the platform. I marvelled at my ability to dissociate myself so soon and so easily from my stint in the forest, from what I had lived through just a few hours back, just as I had dissociated myself from my life on the ship when I set out to look for my sister.

I had dissociated myself from the forest, but why was the fragrance of jamun still lingering around me? Was the fragrance haunting me? My train came, I boarded it, but the fragrance of jamun also boarded with me.

At night, I opened my bag to pull out a sheet. And then I saw it.

A bundle made of leaves, fastened neatly with a string.

I loosened the string and looked inside the bundle. Jamuns.

Ripe, plump jamuns.

Silence knew how much I loved jamuns. This was her farewell gift to me. She had left me the fruit I loved so much.

I put one jamun into my mouth, and when I was done sucking its pulp and only the seed remained, a thought crossed my mind. In the midst of all that violence and destruction, love had managed to survive.

Part 2

# The Ocean

CHAPTER 9

# Export

Jaldoot, our ship, departed from the port at Vishakhapatnam. Instead of socialising with my colleagues, which would have been the obvious thing to do, I went straight to the engine room, where I stood amidst the din of machines and generators. I stood there till the thudding of the machinery and the pulsation of blood in my veins and arteries were fully synchronised with one another. I stood there till the odour of diesel and machine oil had mixed with my breath. I stood there till I turned into a curious entity which was half-Adivasi and half-android.

Once I had become that entity, I went up to the deck of the ship. The ship had left the coast of Andhra Pradesh far behind. Jaldoot was, this time, loaded with containers of iron ore. I wondered which other cargo it had transported in the six months that I wasn't sailing. The iron ore, I came to know, had been mined in Bailadila Hills and was being transported to Japan.

The port at Nagasaki was our destination. This time, my focus wasn't on the machinery aspect of the ship; I was more concerned with the cargo. As the containers of iron ore were being unloaded at Nagasaki, I realised that there was a spike in import and export activities in the coastal areas of Asia. There was a rush especially at the ports in China and Japan, with Japan concentrating on imports and China on exports.

I wouldn't have been interested in the cargo—I wasn't, the last time. I was just an engineer, so the machinery of the ship was what I was primarily concerned with. However, now that I was aware of the cargo and the circumstances under which I had gained that information, I had, even if unduly, become interested in the cargo. I learnt that several shipping companies that had been running at a loss for a long time had been revived in the last three years because of the business transactions they were doing with China. It was being called a golden era for maritime trade in Asia. This wave of economic development which had risen so high, how long would it be before it crashed? And what would happen after it crashed?

The crash did not take too long. Its first ripples were felt while we were still docked in Nagasaki. The golden era spanning the last three years seemed to have come to an end. We were informed that our scheduled journey from Nagasaki to Shanghai had been cancelled. This wasn't due to the weather or because the ship malfunctioned; it happened because the import-export firm with which our shipping company had a contract had gone bankrupt.

Seven days had passed since we docked at the port in Nagasaki. We had played as many rounds of cards and chess as we could in these seven days. Now there was nothing left for us to do or explore. Ennui had set in.

Jaldoot appeared sad when I saw it from the outside. Inside the ship, Captain Alok Datt confined himself to his cabin. It was hard to understand what he did there or what dilemmas plagued his mind. All we got to see was his irritation and irascibility. He had turned stubborn and quite intolerant to our presence and words. Either he appeared lost or he responded furiously to even the smallest occurrences. Gradually, the staff started avoiding him. They tried their best not to appear in his presence and, if somehow, they crossed paths with him and he said something, they just nodded obediently and walked away. The crew still had a lot of regard for Captain Datt. No one spoke ill of him, nor did they mind his brusqueness, but living with him had become akin to living with a terminally ill person.

The ocean engulfs not only the ships that sail on it but also the humans who sail on those ships. Rust eats into not only those objects of iron which aren't being used but also the people who haven't been able to stay in sync with the world. Captain Alok Datt, from what I knew, hadn't set foot on earth for the last three years. His cabin on Jaldoot was his home and, possibly, tomb as well.

## CHAPTER 10

# Carnival

We remained docked in Nagasaki for fifteen days, after which the ship set sail for Shanghai. This time, it was empty. There was no cargo to carry. There were no containers on its deck, nor anything in its cargo hold. It was the first time that the crew were sailing an empty ship from one port to another. Everybody seemed worried by this, but no one could muster the courage to ask Captain Alok Datt what was actually happening. They all felt that it was inauspicious to sail an empty ship.

I found Captain Datt standing on the deck one night, hands on the railing. I went and stood beside him, quietly. I knew—and I suppose he knew too—that he would eventually look at me and talk. Perhaps he was waiting for the right moment.

I wondered what he was staring at on the dark surface of the water. Was he looking forward to something? Or did he know that nothing was going to happen and so he was just thinking of what had already happened?

'I'm not upset,' Captain Alok Datt said to me suddenly. 'I already knew what was going to happen.'

I didn't know what he was talking about. What was going to happen? What was he not upset about?

'You're right,' I said. 'Now it remains to be seen what will come of this.'

I had no idea what I was saying. I spoke only out of my regard for Captain Datt, only to make him feel that he wasn't alone in this conversation.

He nodded at my words and said, 'No one cares for old things. What is old is either abandoned or broken down.'

I couldn't make head or tail of his words. Which old things was he talking about? It seemed like he was talking of something familiar, but what was it? Yet, I said, 'Yes, it's sad that old things aren't valued.'

'Hmm ...' He rubbed his beard and adopted a thoughtful stance. 'I don't think there will be any stopping this time.'

He seemed lost in his thoughts. I said nothing, just waited for him to shake out of the reverie and speak—and he soon did.

'The ship is being taken back today,' he said without looking at me, 'like cattle that can neither be milked anymore nor worked on a farm. Such cattle are sent to slaughter houses.'

I stayed mum.

'You know what used to happen earlier?' he asked, his gaze still distant. 'Whenever there was a famine somewhere, ships from one country would carry grains and food to the country affected by the famine, and that saved people from perishing.

Ships are blessed, for they transport things to places where they are most needed.'

I could see that our conversation was moving to grave territories, yet I couldn't understand why Captain Datt was telling me all this. As if on an impulse, my hand went into my pocket and grabbed Passion.

'I have studied genocides in which millions of people were put to death outright,' he said. 'Genocides are still occurring, but they don't appear to be genocides prima facie now. The days of Hitler-like barbarism are over. Inflation determines the violence now. Ripped, crumpled paper thrown into the garbage on Wall Street may show which country has been destroyed today.'

I clutched Passion tightly in my fist but, much to my surprise, Passion did not respond. I began rubbing it, as if it were some magical stone or lamp. I patted it, as if waking a sleeping child. I mumbled in my mind for Passion to work. I tried to telepathically communicate with Passion. Nothing worked. Passion did not show me anything that might help me understand what Captain Alok Datt was speaking about.

He changed his position. Turning around, he rested his back against the railing. Now he was facing the wide, empty deck of the ship, gazing at it studiously. His gaze suggested that the deck of Jaldoot had turned into a stage for something momentous. Perhaps he was able to see what was imminent. But what was it that Captain Datt was able to see? What was going on in his mind?

The narrative that followed was divided into three acts, all three telling stories of violence of different types. The first was racial violence; the second, violence borne out of differences based on caste and religion; and the third was economic violence. Captain Datt thought that the violence instigated by wealth did not discriminate. It affected all, regardless of the victim's religion, caste or race.

'I was sixteen years old when my father, Mohan Datt, told me about what he had witnessed when he was sixteen,' Captain Alok Datt began. 'My grandfather, Prahlad Datt, was based in West Virginia in America at the time. He was a prominent merchant of dry fruits and his business was spread across several states. Once, he travelled to Ohio to deal with a matter related to the purchase of almonds. He took my father with him. They were being driven in their vintage car by their driver who was Mexican, an immigrant like they themselves were.

'My father, Mohan Datt, was sixteen years old at the time. On the way, there was a town which was famous for its annual Lynching Carnival. My father wasn't aware of the carnival, but his father knew what it was all about. He was urging the driver to take them out of that town as soon as possible. But as luck would have it, their car broke down some three or four kilometres before the town.

'It was the day of the carnival, so garages were closed. There was no mechanic to be found. They had to leave their car on the road and walk. They had walked some distance when they came across a flock of people going to the carnival. There were men and women in vehicles, cheering, shouting excitedly.

'When my father and grandfather reached the town, they found all its shops closed. Even offices and schools were closed. Both father and son were trapped in the crowd of merrymakers, being pushed towards the carnival ground. There were food stalls along the road. There were posters of lynching on every wall.

'A shiver ran down my father's spine on seeing the posters. For on them were images of mutilated bodies of the Black people who had been massacred in previous carnivals. My grandfather stood between my father and those posters. But for how long could he shield his son from what was about to happen there?

'The band started playing and the crowd parted, making way for it. The band entered the carnival ground, followed by a procession. When the procession came closer, my father saw three naked Black men at its head. Their hands were tied behind their backs and they were being whipped.

'The crowd was cheering for the people who were whipping the Black men and also jeering at those who weren't being able to whip them hard enough. The mob looked impatient, as if they would snatch the whips and whip those three men themselves. But they could not do it, for those who were lashing the Black men had bought the right to do so, in keeping with the rules of the carnival, through an auction. The right to whip a Black man was not transferable.

'A few special trains had been run for the carnival. Crowds of people alighted from a train to participate in it. People were waving hats and clothes from the roofs of houses and shops nearby.

'The cheering and jeering stopped when the three Black men reached the centre of the ground. They were made to stand together and the gathered crowd stood around them in a circle. The organisers of the carnival announced the rules. They hung plates bearing numbers around the necks of those three Black men and invited the spectators to bid to cut off parts of their bodies.

'A few hands rose from among the spectators. But when the organisers began exhorting the crowd, a few more people started bidding. The Black man wearing the plate bearing the number one was dragged forward. The bidding started with his right ear.

'Bidding for the right ear of the Black man numbered one started at one hundred and one dollars. Six people bid. When the bid reached two hundred and one dollars, two people withdrew. When it reached three hundred and one, two more people withdrew. There were only two people left now. One of those two men was tall and burly, but he wasn't adventurous enough to bid a higher amount. The other man was a dwarf, but he bid a higher amount and won the right to cut off the right ear of the Black man.

'The Black man numbered one was tied to a wooden post. The crowd began cheering again. A platter of daggers and knives was placed before the short man who had won the bid. While the dwarf was trying to choose a suitable knife, the crowd cheered, quite unmindful of the difference between the build of the White man and the Black man. When the White man raised the knife he had chosen, it reached only till the shoulder of the Black man. The crowd laughed. The dwarf got annoyed. He tried to swing his arm up to reach the Black man's ear but failed. The crowd laughed again. The burly man who had lost the bid was laughing the loudest, nearly falling to the ground as he laughed. The dwarf tried again and again but failed each time. The crowd laughed louder, the burly man laughing the loudest. That annoyed the dwarf even more.

'The Black man was watching the entire show with a certain calm. He was terrified, no doubt, but he had perhaps resigned himself to his fate. When the dwarf failed in all his attempts at reaching the Black man's ear, a smile spread on the Black man's face. An insulting, hateful smile. Soon, that smile turned into a loud, throaty laughter.

'That was the last straw. The dwarf summoned an organiser, asked him to go on all fours, climbed on his back and, in one fell swoop, slashed the Black man's ear with the knife. The Black man howled in pain as his right ear fell to the ground.

'The crowd went silent. But a moment later, the cheering began again, louder and crazier than before.

'It was just the beginning. Gradually, bidding took place for the other ear and other body parts, all of which were hacked off. The same happened to the second and the third Black men. What remained on the ground were dismembered body parts of three dead men still tied to the wooden posts.

'Champagne bottles were popped. Men and women cheered loudly. People stuffed themselves with food as if they were not at the site of a lynching but at a wedding feast. White supremacy was being celebrated.

'My grandfather and father were not a part of that celebration, but they could not leave the town till the carnival ended. They were not Black, nor were they White. Their very presence there seemed like an abomination. But there was nothing they could do. Like the Whites, they had to move on to the final stage of the carnival.

'The final stage involved putting on display the slashed body parts of the three Black men on a wall outside the town hall. There was music, there was noise, the crowd was proudly watching the display, but my grandfather and father did not dare look up at the wall. That was when someone from the cheering crowd held them from behind and turned them towards the wall. They saw before them a pair of buttocks and an earless and noseless head above the buttocks. A penis was thrust into the opening from where the mouth had been cut. Ten fingers decorated the head.

'The carnival ended and father and son came out of the town hall compound. They said nothing to each other, but the son perhaps understood what was on his father's mind. They returned to the car and somehow, with the help of the driver, had it repaired. Their driver, a Mexican, an outsider, perhaps understood what was going on in his employer's mind.

'My grandfather told his driver to take them back to West Virginia. Upon returning home, he began folding up his business. It took some days, but he did it quickly enough. He told my grandmother to pack all their things. In a little over a week, dry fruit merchant Prahlad Datt, together with his wife, their five daughters and son, was on board a ship that would take them back to Asia. They left the United States of America for good.'

## CHAPTER 11

# Division

Captain Alok Datt's story flashed before my eyes like a showreel. Now I understood why he was the way he was, why he thought the way he did, why he was a loner, why he roamed the ship's deck at night.

'What happened after that?' I was so curious to know more about the return of Captain Alok Datt's family that I asked the question immediately, quite unmindful of his state of mind.

Captain Datt said nothing. He went to the stairs and, holding the rails, started climbing down towards the cabins, slowly, wearily. He went to his cabin and shut the door behind him.

I remained standing outside his cabin. I didn't know what else to do; he had never left a conversation so abruptly before. It took me a while to decide whether to remain there or leave.

I didn't have to arrive at a decision, for the door to Captain Datt's cabin opened soon after. He held a glass of liquor in his hand. He looked at me for some time. I lowered my gaze. He stepped back from the door and went inside. Was he inviting me to come in? Was he angry with me for standing outside his cabin? I couldn't gauge the situation. But considering that he could have shut the door in my face had he been angry with me, I took the open door as an invitation and walked into the cabin.

The cabin was stuffy, and it made me nauseous, but after a while, I got used to it. He poured me a drink and we sat down beside his table. He began to tell the rest of the story.

The ship brought Prahlad Datt and his family to the port at Karachi in pre-partition Pakistan. When all their luggage had been brought off the ship, Prahlad Datt placed his hand on Mohan Datt's shoulder. That moment infused a sense of responsibility into Mohan Datt. He asked his father, 'Where do we go from here?'

'We'll go to Rawalpindi first,' Prahlad Datt told his son. 'There is a village called Peryaraizada near Rawalpindi. Several of our relatives and acquaintances live there.'

'What will we do in Peryaraizada?'

'We'll consult with our relatives on business matters, where we should live, which business we should invest in.'

They travelled from Karachi to Rawalpindi by train. At the railway station in Rawalpindi, Prahlad Datt handed his briefcase, in which he kept documents related to his business, to his son. Mohan Datt was hesitant, he couldn't shoulder the responsibility of his father's business so soon. But, once again, his father placed his hand on his shoulder. Mohan Datt took the briefcase from his father's hand and took a look at the wide, new world that lay before him. On coming out of the railway station, he held out his index finger to his youngest sister. The little girl, who had so far held only her father's finger, grabbed his index finger and started walking with him.

A rented jeep brought the family to a village not very far from Peryaraizada. Raizada Tribhowandas, Prahlad Datt's father-in-law, received them warmly. Prahlad Datt had wanted to go first to the paternal side of his family in Peryaraizada, to his cousins, but the village of his in-laws was on the way, and when his father-in-law came to know that they were travelling that way, he had invited them to stay.

The next few days were spent talking about business matters. This was the first time Mohan Datt was visiting his mother's family. It impressed him to no end to find that he came from an illustrious line of ancestors. They were Mohyal Brahmins, also known as Hussaini Brahmins, and they were, despite being Hindu—and Brahmins, at that—highly revered among the Shia Muslims, for history had it that a Mohyal Brahmin had fought alongside Imam al-Husayn in the battle of Karbala, even sacrificing his seven sons.

However, the battle of Karbala had been fought centuries ago. They were in the year 1942. The fight for Independence was on and the fear of partition loomed large. India's partition meant a division between Hindus and Muslims. The Hussaini Brahmins were worried, for they were somewhere midway between Hindus and Muslims. In the event of a partition, where would they go? Which side would they take?

Prahlad Datt and Mohan Datt had, in their adopted home, witnessed the differences between the White race and the Black race. In India, their own land, a world of differences between Hindus and Muslims cropped up before them. Built out of two faiths, Hinduism and Islam, where would the Mohyal Muslims go if there was a partition?

Mohan Datt, all of sixteen, could sense the chaos. Would it be right to start a business in this atmosphere, he wondered. Despite getting proposals for investment from several parties, Mohan Datt felt safer depositing his father's hard-earned money in a bank.

They stayed at Raizada Tribhowandas's house for two weeks, after which they rented a house outside the village. After setting up the household, Mohan Datt decided to focus on his sisters' education. The village did not have a good school, but there was a convent school some distance away. Mohan Datt felt he could afford to send his sisters there. They would have to cut corners, but the family would have the basic comforts.

Prahlad Datt supported his son's decision. Mohan Datt looked proudly at his five sisters as they put on their school uniforms and climbed into a horse-drawn tonga to go to their new school.

Some time passed. The family settled into a routine. One night, after they had finished dinner, Mohan Datt spoke to his father about resuming business. Prahlad Datt too was eager to start working. While his son was busy setting up the household, he visited the wholesale market in Rawalpindi. The seasoned dry fruit merchant that he was, he smelt opportunities in the market. The scale of trade in pistachio, fig, dates, walnut and almond was large. However, most traders here had no ties with big buyers in places like Delhi, Bombay and Karachi. These big buyers had to purchase their goods through middlemen. By the time the goods reached the markets in Delhi, Bombay and Karachi, after passing through middlemen and commission agents, their prices shot up.

Father and son decided to develop new ways of marketing and also protecting their merchandise from riots in case any happened in the future.

The first step was to rent a godown instead of opening a shop in the market. They purchased goods from the markets in Afghanistan and stored their merchandise in their godown in Rawalpindi. At the godown, they packed their merchandise in small packages, intended to be sold directly to retailers. This was a very American way of doing business.

Once they came to understand the transportation network, their business took off. They did away with middlemen, so they were able to pay the dry fruit growers better than the other traders. Their plan worked and, very soon, Prahlad Datt and Mohan Datt started making profits.

There were tribal groups, like the Pathans, that were involved in the dry fruit trade. They still followed their age-old ways of trading and were not averse to killing their adversaries. These producers of dry fruits had to transport their goods on mules. On their journey, they had to stop at roadside inns run by men of the Sayyad caste. At those inns, the growers of dry fruits were frequently robbed, sometimes even at the hands of the innkeepers. As such, the growers of dry fruits had to deal with tribal chiefs, innkeepers and, finally, the Hindu traders of the Baniya caste who paid quite a low price for the goods.

When Messrs Datt Dry Fruit Company started capturing the market, the Pathans, Sayyads and Baniyas could not understand what had hit them. They couldn't understand how the goods were getting sold even before they had arrived at the market. By the time they learnt of the devices adopted by Messrs Datt Dry Fruit Company, the first shipment of that season's produce had left for Bombay via the port at Karachi and for Delhi via Pathankot.

Prahlad Datt, the visionary that he was, had already insured his godown and signed contracts with the transport companies. Most of the transport companies were operated by Sikhs, who were quite the fighters themselves and knew how to defend their shipments and transport them safely to their intended destinations.

The business aspect of the lives of the Datts was now sorted, but there were other pressing issues too. Those were chaotic times. Violence was on the rise in villages. Houses belonging to Hindus and Sikhs were being burned and women were being forcefully carried away. Hindu and Sikh families were leaving their villages en masse. There was news about people attempting to escape to the Punjab but being killed on the way; the women were kidnapped and brutalised.

The committee of Mohyal Brahmins in the village of Peryaraizada called a meeting one day where the elders decided they should all leave. The Muslims in Peryaraizada had, so far, treated them with respect and they had no reason to fear them; but times were changing and so were the attitudes of people. They did not think that the Muslims remembered any longer the sacrifices the Mohyal Brahmins had made in the battle of Karbala. The Hussaini part of their Hussaini

Brahmin identity was getting eroded and now they were only Brahmins—that is, Hindu.

Captain Alok Datt paused at that point. I looked at the clock in his cabin. It was a quarter past midnight. The bottle of liquor was half empty. The remaining alcohol swayed inside the bottle as the ship rocked over the waves in the ocean. It would be some time before both got over: the liquor and Captain Datt's story. There was no hurry, no urgency.

For some time, Captain Datt sat still, like a meditating hermit. Then, stroking his beard, he picked up his glass. As if his voice was emerging from a deep well of thoughts, he said, 'How long could a man wander and how many times could he save himself?'

I was staring at the books on the captain's table. Upon hearing his voice, I looked up at him. He took a long draught from his glass. 'What has to happen will happen,' he said conclusively. 'One can often foresee what's going to happen. But events don't always follow man's conjectures. Sometimes the unthinkable happens.'

'I don't understand,' I said, a bit loudly, more to reassure him that I was paying attention than for any other reason.

'When one's own life and the lives of one's loved ones are at stake, a man can go to any lengths.'

He began telling the rest of the story.

'It was a maddening time. Acts of violence and barbarism from that time have gone down in the annals of history. People of one community butchered people from the other community. In some families, however, the killings were not done by rioters from another community but by their own elders for fear of their women being raped and dishonoured. So they themselves put the women to death. Blood from the bodies of minor girls and daughters-in-law was splattered on the walls of their houses, but their deaths were never spoken of. Twenty-seven women were killed in my grandfather's village during the partition by their own fathers or fathers-in-law.'

Captain Datt finished the liquor remaining in his glass and put it back on the table with a thud. Then he lit a cigarette and drew a puff.

'That day, my father was not in the village,' he said, exhaling smoke. 'He was in Rawalpindi.'

I listened attentively.

'My father stood before the godown of Messrs Datt Dry Fruit Company, which had been set on fire. There was black smoke rising from the godown, and also from several other shops, houses, Hindu temples and gurdwaras. Then he encountered a mob which was more savage than the one he had witnessed at the Lynching Carnival in America. At the Lynching Carnival, only three men were dismembered and put to death following the rules and regulations of the event, whereas in the riot in Rawalpindi, sixty Sikh men were lined up, stripped naked, their hair cut off, and their heads chopped off. The cut heads were then thrown and kicked around on the ground. Their genitals were hacked, put into a copper urn and carried out in a procession.

'My father hid behind a house and let the killer procession pass. When the roads were clear, he came out of hiding. He found a bicycle left behind by a man who had been butchered by the mob. He picked up the bicycle and pedalled back to the village.

'He returned to find the village empty. There was no sign anywhere of violence or killing, but the desolation alone was unsettling and frightening.

'My father turned into the lane that led towards his house. It was deserted. He passed by a neighbouring house where a cow, tethered to a stump, was bellowing. There was an elderly man lying on a cot, warding off flies from his face. My father went near the old man and asked, "Where is everyone?" The old man said, "They've gone to the nearby village of Pind Sayyada."

'My father remembered that the Sayyads from Pind Sayyada had once been invited to a meeting of the Mohyal Brahmins in Peryaraizada. The Sayyads had taken a vow to shelter the Mohyal Brahmins if they came to harm.

'My father heaved a sigh of relief. He knew that there were Mohyal Brahmin families in the village who had unwavering faith in the Sayyads, even though he could not understand how a handful of Sayyads would be able to protect them if an army of rioters descended on the village. Yet, he relaxed, believing that his family was safe.

'He pedalled on to Pind Sayyada. There was a festival-like atmosphere in that village. Pandals had been put up in open spaces and communal meals were being served. The Sayyads of the village had received the Mohyal Brahmins warmly and didn't leave any stone unturned in making them feel safe and at home. Young Sayyad men, dressed in shalwar-kurta and with the customary Sayyadi turban on their heads, were obeying their elders and taking good care of their guests.

'My father looked inside the men's tent, but he couldn't find his father there. When he asked people about him, they just shook their heads. But my father was perceptive enough to understand that they were hiding something from him. He dashed towards the women's tent to look for his mother and sisters. He was anxious and panting as he looked around. He finally found his mother inside a house. She was surrounded by women who were consoling her.

'My grandmother stood up on seeing my father. The women made way for her to walk towards her son. Both mother and son stood facing each other, neither saying a word.

'"Where is Pitaji?" My father broke the silence.

'Tears flowed from my grandmother's eyes.

'"My sisters?" he asked.

'His mother broke down then.

'My father lost no time. He grabbed that unknown man's bicycle and pedalled like a storm back to his own village. In his impatience, he had missed looking into his own house. Now he forgot to breathe; all his senses propelled him towards his house.

'He rode into the compound, saw the sight there, and fell off the bicycle. Leaves from the peepal tree in the yard fell upon him, and two crows cawed inauspiciously from somewhere among the branches. His sisters' school uniforms swayed in the wind. My father walked straight, as if in a trance, towards the basin built in the yard for storing water. There were flies hovering over it. My father peered in. The basin was filled with blood. Some of it had congealed and turned into clots. There were five bodies beneath that layer of clotted blood.

'He couldn't look anymore. He stepped back, blank, unable to speak, unable to think, even unable to grieve.

'When he returned to his senses after some time, he thought of his father. Where was his father?

'He walked across the compound towards the door of the house, which was latched from the inside. He knocked thrice on the door with the iron chain hanging on it. The door opened a while later. My father was now prepared for almost anything.

'His father's clothes and hands were smeared with blood. His face, like his son's, was blank.

'Father and son stood facing each other in the middle of a divided world. But they weren't looking at that divided world. They were looking at each other. Against the background of black smoke rising from houses engulfed in red flames and flies hovering over the bodies of chopped up men and women, the father and the son looked at each other's faces.'

'My boy.' Captain Datt stood up, walked towards me and placed his hand on my shoulder. 'I don't know why I told you my story. When I first saw you, I saw a part of me in you. As if you too were built to witness destruction of a colossal magnitude.'

I looked into his grey eyes, and kept looking for a long time till he averted his gaze. I turned my gaze towards the books on his table and pulled one out of the stack. I was shocked to read its title, so shocked I felt the alcohol wear off me. I placed the book back into the stack and pulled out another one. I felt dizzy. All the books on Captain Datt's table dealt with one massacre or the other.

I turned to look at him. He was reclining in his chair, fast asleep. I felt like lifting him up and carrying him to his bed. But I didn't, for I was afraid I might wake him up. So I just covered him with a blanket and came out of his cabin.

I went straight to the deck and looked towards the east. The sun was rising from somewhere afar. Birds were already out in the sky, flying. How pleasant was that sight! How innocent, after hearing the frightening stories in Captain Datt's cabin.

'Dawn, you're very beautiful,' I said suddenly. I don't know why.

Our ship docked at the port in Shanghai an hour or so after midday. Captain Alok Datt came out of his cabin, dressed immaculately in a clean uniform. He had his back towards all of us. Before us, before Captain Alok Datt, was the dazzling infrastructure of Shanghai, glaring arrogantly at the world.

Captain Datt walked down the gangway and went to the office of the shipping company. I kept looking at him as he turned into a speck in the distance and finally disappeared. Then I yawned, returned to my cabin, threw myself on the bed and fell asleep.

When I woke up, I saw the golden rays of the sun bouncing off the East China Sea. I looked out of the window at the ships in the distance. Then I went to the washbasin and splashed water on my face. After wiping my face and neck with a towel, I examined my reflection in the mirror.

'What is it?' I asked my reflection.

My reflection shook his head. 'Nothing,' it said.

'Then why do you look so glum?'

My reflection said nothing.

'Can you ever become a man with a willpower and a sense of self-worth?' I asked.

'I cannot play into a stereotype,' my reflection shot back.

'Stereotype?'

'Yes, stereotype. You think you can fool others by appearing to be melancholy and self-absorbed?'

'Do you know what you're saying?'

'I know very well. But it seems you have lost yourself. Do you even know who you are?'

His words annoyed me.

'Are you all right?' he asked in mock concern. 'It seems you've seen a ghost.'

I turned around and walked into the toilet. I stripped naked and sat on the commode. I could feel my heart beating against my chest as the words my reflection had spoken rolled tumultuously inside my head.

CHAPTER 12

# Aid

The last of the sun's rays were diminishing when I reached the deck. I saw my co-workers sitting on chairs in a circle in the middle of the deck. Mr Shafi, the chief engineer, and Madan Mehta, the incharge of the control room, were talking to each other, while the others sipped tea and listened to them. I too sat down with a cup of tea in my hand, but I wasn't interested in the conversation; I was looking at the dark clouds looming over the Shanghai skyline.

Against that inky background, we saw Captain Alok Datt panting as he walked over the gangway to the ship. He wasn't as sprightly as he had been in the morning. The knot of his tie was loose, he held his cap in his hand, his shirt was untucked and was flapping in the wind, even his hair was scruffy and blowing in the wind. He tottered towards us on the deck. As he came closer, we all stood up. He gestured at us to remain seated. I offered my chair to him, but he only held on to it for balance.

'I cannot guarantee anything,' he said between laboured breaths. 'The queue is just too long.' He pointed towards the port where several ships were anchored in a row.

'But what has happened?' Madan Mehta stood up and asked anxiously. 'Why has the loading been stopped? Is there a storm coming? Is there going to be a war? What has happened?'

'It's more serious than that.' Captain Datt looked at Madan Mehta. 'The global economy has crashed. Thailand and Japan have devalued their currencies. There's high inflation. Other countries too may revise their exchange rates. This storm is deadlier than any storm at sea, and ships usually do not survive such a storm.'

The crowd stood dumbstruck upon hearing the captain's words.

'Why have you all turned so silent?' Captain Datt said, trying to cheer us up. 'There are troubles everywhere. All troubles can be resolved. This one too shall be resolved.'

Captain Datt's words did not appear to have an effect on anyone. Chief Engineer Shafi stood up and asked, firmly but calmly, 'Captain, we know these matters are not in your hands. We just want to know what's been decided in the meeting at the shipping company's office?'

Captain Datt was at a loss for words. He turned away from Mr Shafi and fixed his gaze somewhere far on the horizon. He appeared worried. Then, turning towards us, eyes lowered, he said to no one in particular, 'Our shipping company does not have any work now. Our contract's been cancelled. We are going to return.'

Then, without hesitating anymore, he ordered for the anchor to be lifted.

All of us looked at him in stunned silence. Then everyone got down to doing the tasks that needed to be done in order to sail away. I looked at the Shanghai shoreline for some time. Then I too moved away.

I walked to the deck and watched the clouds in the fading glow of the setting sun. Our situation was uncertain, but I wasn't as agitated as the others, even though I should have been worried, for my job too was at stake. I tried feeling something, anything, but I couldn't. I realised later that I'd spent two hours on the deck, holding on to the railing, trying to stir some feeling within me. I would have kept on standing there, had it not been for an angry, agitated voice. The voice came from the dining hall and it was followed by the sound of bottles, glasses and other crockery being flung to the ground.

On my way to the dining hall, I heard the agitated voices of people raising an alarm and trying to pacify someone who was clearly angry. When I got there, I saw a flock of people surrounding Mr Shafi, who was blabbering something about the policies of Grand Eastern Shipping Company. I had never seen him angry, ever. He was known to be a gentleman, calm and refined. I remembered the incident from our last trip when he had offered to help me fix the generators. But today, his hair was unkempt, he had thrown his spectacles somewhere, and his eyes glowed in anger. Madan Mehta and another member from the crew were holding his arms, trying to restrain him. A seaman and two technicians, who had climbed up to the dining hall, stood cautiously before him, lest he do something untoward. The rest of the men there had been caught unawares between their meal; they were gaping at Mr Shafi, wondering what had come over him.

Madan Mehta said something to Mr Shafi, perhaps something soothing to calm his nerves, but Mr Shafi just shrugged off his arm. I walked closer and stood before Mr Shafi. His anger remained unabated. All six of us stood surrounding Mr Shafi without saying a word. We just stood and waited.

Mr Shafi calmed down after some time. I held him and slowly nudged him to the same corner in the dining hall where, on our last trip, Captain Alok Datt and I had sat down. I made him sit on the same chair in which Captain Alok Datt had sat. A steward came and placed Mr Shafi's spectacles on the table between us and returned to clear the shards of broken crockery from the floor.

The spectacles were safe, the lenses undamaged. Mr Shafi sat still for some time, not speaking, just staring at the table. Then he took out his handkerchief and, wiping his glasses, he placed them back on the table. Then he wiped the sweat off his face, put his handkerchief away, wore his spectacles, and began looking out of the window. I couldn't tell what he was looking at, for it was dark outside. But he was calm, and that was what mattered.

A while later, I saw raindrops rolling down the glass of the window. I went to the buffet and brought two bowls of soup. Mr Shafi glanced scornfully at the soup and turned again towards the window. It was as if he wasn't looking outside the window but merely avoiding looking at what was inside. After some time, though, he drank a few spoonfuls of the soup. Then he pushed the bowl away, stood up, and left the dining hall without stopping to speak to anyone.

After finishing dinner, I went up to the deck. I stood at the same spot where I had seen Captain Datt on my first journey aboard Jaldoot. That was where he had initiated me into his world. This was perhaps our last journey together. Something inside me said I would meet Captain Datt here again. I had a hunch that he had left something unsaid, so he would surely return to this spot on the deck. It could also end up being our final conversation.

I heard familiar footsteps climbing up the stairs to the deck. I turned around to face Captain Datt. Unlike other times, he did not place his hand on my shoulder. I knew he was looking at me, but I couldn't see his face, for I was blinded by the lights from the ship's tower. I could only see his hair fluttering under his navy cap.

We stood in silence for a few minutes, both of us holding on to the railing and looking out into the sea in the darkness. Then he began speaking.

'I told you two stories of violence that my father told me,' he said, his eyes still on the dark vastness of the sea. 'But there is also a third kind of violence that I'm going to tell you about now. In this tale of violence, there is no bloodshed, but there is killing, there are deaths.'

Captain Alok Datt's words did not immediately make sense to me, but he continued to speak. He was just hurling details at me. Details and anecdotes. I had no way of verifying the veracity of the stories he told me. But I don't think he was at all concerned about that, for his mind was imploding. He was just raring to pour it all out.

Captain Datt took me thirty years back in time, to Ethiopia. Thousands of emaciated, hungry bodies dotted a drought-stricken landmass. Hundreds of corpses lay waiting, in want of shrouds and burial.

I couldn't understand what bearing a drought in Ethiopia all those years ago had on the economic depression we were facing now. When Captain Datt recounted a story or an anecdote, he didn't establish relevance; he was only concerned with the narration. It was up to the listener to deduce its relevance or form a conclusion.

I was concerned for Captain Datt. I think I had spotted that point in his subconscious from where he seemed to travel into a different world, lower himself down to unknown depths, lose himself in an uncertain mist from where he remained disconnected from the real, tangible world outside.

I was afraid that Captain Datt might not return from the other world, might not be able to haul himself out of those unknown depths, that he might not be able to find his way out of that uncertain mist. But what could I do about my worry for him? Could I help in any way? Could I tell him anything? Would he listen to me? Perhaps, no. The only thing I could do was listen to him, hear him out, indulge him as he poured his heart out to me.

Through Captain Alok Datt's recounting, I saw donations and allies heading towards Ethiopia.

'Mercy and financial aid too are types of violence,' he said.

'The land is tainted with bloodshed,' he continued. 'I chose the sea and ships so that I wouldn't have to see the savagery rampant on land. But I didn't know that ships were built for just that: violence. Ships were built so that unknown lands could be discovered, so that those lands could be branded as uncivilised and ravaged under the pretext of civilisation. And when that entire land had been destroyed and was faced with droughts and calamities, those same ships would be used to send aid and further imprison it. The people working on those ships often did not know what cargo mined from which destitute nation they were carrying, for all that was decided by powers much bigger than all of us.'

I don't recall when, during the course of our conversation, we climbed down the deck and went inside Captain Alok Datt's cabin. We sat at the same table where he had told me the story of racial violence in America and the story of communal violence in undivided India. He now told me a story of economic violence.

Captain Datt told me that he used to work with the Mediterranean Shipping Co. in Denmark. Their ships used to carry dairy products from Denmark to Ethiopia and return with timber of Eucalyptus trees.

'I had no idea at the time about the timber that was traded,' Captain Datt said, pouring out his third glass of liquor and dusting his cigarette in the ashtray.

'It's all rubbish, the research that professional researchers and historians have done on Ethiopia. This research is at the heart of a Eurocentric history. It is hard to fathom why one feels the need to understand Africa through the European gaze. Africa can be understood only through African voices. European historians wasted hundreds of pages to prove that the famine in Ethiopia was a natural calamity, while the real reasons were conveniently kept out of their books and research papers.'

Captain Datt took a long drag on his cigarette and stubbed it out in the ashtray.

'I spoke to the labourers at a port in Ethiopia. They used to be farmers. They told me that Eucalyptus trees have fifty times more capacity than other trees to soak up and hold the moisture in the earth. That is why, earlier, Eucalyptus trees were grown only in waterlogged, marshy land to suck the surplus water and make the land suitable for farming. But there were hardly any marshes in Ethiopia. Yet, plantation companies with their origins in corporate houses in the West planted Eucalyptus trees on thousands of hectares of land in Ethiopia. It was an industrial crop, and no one in Ethiopia knew at the time what havoc it would wreak.'

Captain Alok Datt lit one more cigarette.

'In the next fifteen years, those plantation companies completely destroyed the agricultural land in Ethiopia. Eucalyptus trees sucked up every last drop of water in the land. The timber traders harvested their crop and went away. Nothing could ever be grown again in the farmlands of Ethiopia.'

Captain Datt did not say anything after that and remained lost in thought. I too looked out of the window quietly. But even in that darkness, I could see the arid landmass of Ethiopia and thousands of children wailing in hunger. And then I saw the relief camps of Bastar. I saw the hills of Bailadila. I saw mines. I saw the logos of international corporate houses. I saw trains carrying iron ore and other minerals to the port at Vishakhapatnam. I saw ships carrying this cargo out to sea. Was mining in Bastar the same as planting Eucalyptus trees in Ethiopia where they were not needed at all? Images of hollow mines and arid fields disturbed me. I felt something crumbling within me. I felt something mining me. And what seemed to emerge from that mining was an understanding of why thousands of people in Bastar were fighting against the mining companies and why the government was fighting those people back.

I wondered if I was drunk. I took a deep breath and looked at Captain Datt. He looked back at me and shook his head in a defeated way.

'I know that I may be wrong,' he said. 'I accept that I do not have full knowledge of many issues. But what can I do? I cannot help thinking about such issues. I am, after all, just a seaman. And issues, like waves in an ocean, toss me here and there, make me restless.'

Captain Datt paused awhile and then looked at me again.

'I wish I were a sociologist, or an academic. I wish I knew the right words. I wish I knew how to string my thoughts together and express myself better. Then perhaps I could have explained to you in an easier way how the acts of violence in one's past, which were marked by bloodshed, are different from this modern form of violence. The violence perpetrated in wars and battles, the weapons which were used—from daggers and the guillotine and noose to nuclear bombs—they were all visible. Swords, spears, guns, cannons—they were all visible, they all had identifiable forms of their own. The people who used them had a form too. They were identified as enemies, as invaders. The people who were killed at their hands too had identities. Their deaths were counted, their martyrdom was acknowledged. But if you think of the violence being perpetrated nowadays, where are the invaders? They invade, they kill, they plunder, but are they ever seen as invaders? Does anyone call them plunderers? And those who are killed at their hands, are their deaths accounted for? Are their deaths even acknowledged?'

I rested my elbows on the table and grabbed my head with both my hands. I was certain now that Captain Alok Datt had entered an abyss inside his head. It wouldn't be possible to bring him back again so soon. But how could I bear his tirade, which I did not entirely understand, and anyway, I had no idea what good it would do me or anyone else to understand it?

Captain Alok Datt stared at the wall behind me, a glowing cigarette clenched between his teeth. A line of smoke emanated from its burning end and blew upwards, between his eyes, which were red with anger.

'I worked with the Mediterranean Shipping Co. for ten years. On my last trip with the company, when our ship sailed from Denmark, I was very excited. I felt that I was part of a meaningful expedition. After all, our ship was loaded with thousands of tons of butter and powdered milk which were being sent in aid to the famine-stricken people and malnourished children of Ethiopia. The UNICEF flag flew beside the national flag of Denmark at the top of our ship. I proudly saluted both the flags. I was very happy, very proud. Before that journey, I had seen our ship doing only trade. This was the first time that I was on a humanitarian mission. But I was so wrong, just so wrong. I didn't know that instead of human mercy, I was going to witness a new form of violence.'

I was bored by now. Unlike other times, Captain Datt's words seemed too heavy-handed. I wondered why he wasn't coming straight to the point. What was the use of a preamble so long-drawn?

The liquor left in the bottle wasn't enough for two people. I picked it up and poured all of it into Captain Datt's glass, keeping the bottle tilted over the glass till the last drop had fallen.

'I wonder why the captain of a cargo ship should be so concerned with violence, economic or otherwise?' I asked and immediately regretted it.

Captain Datt was stunned by my sudden, spontaneous question. He glared at me. Then he hobbled out of his cabin. I hurriedly followed him.

He walked towards the deck. I rushed after him. I saw that the weather had taken a turn for the worse. A storm came and it began to rain heavily. I wondered why I hadn't heard the storm while I was in the captain's cabin. It wasn't like I was engrossed in his monologue. Was I drunk then? Or was it that even though I wasn't interested in his story, I couldn't help paying attention to it?

The storm was a wild one, and Captain Datt was heavily inebriated. He staggered as he climbed the stairs up to the deck where the rain was pelting down. I held him, trying to keep him from falling, but he shrugged my hand away and climbed to the deck.

The downpour drenched both of us. Yet, Captain Datt, undeterred, walked to the same spot on the deck where he usually stood. He held the railing and looked at the stormy sea. I ran and stood beside him, holding on to the railing.

'They threw all the powdered milk and butter into the sea,' I heard Captain Datt mumble. His eyes were still on the sea.

'They stopped our ship some nautical miles away from the port in Ethiopia and dumped all the powdered milk and butter into the sea. If they were distributed free, as aid, in Ethiopia, they felt that the value of Danish dairy products would depreciate in the world market. And it was necessary for them to sustain the value of those dairy products. What I saw happening in the name of the UNICEF was nothing short of a massacre. I had heard and read about a holocaust driven by race and religion. What I saw off the coast of Ethiopia was a holocaust driven by the economy.'

Captain Datt turned silent. He just kept standing on the deck, holding on to the railing and staring at the sea. A couple of hours must have passed. I too did not move. I couldn't leave him alone on the deck in that state, nor could I muster up the courage to hold him and lead him back to his cabin. So we remained standing there. The rain stopped, the storm passed, our clothes were dry again. The previous night's intoxication wore off, and faint sunlight heralded the arrival of a new day. That's when Captain Datt returned to the present and, without looking at me or saying anything, turned around and hobbled back to his cabin.

My sleep was gone, so instead of returning to my cabin, I went straight to the engine room. I worked through the day, went to the dining hall around sunset, ate my fill, and then went to my cabin and fell asleep immediately.

My sleep broke quite early the next morning. In fact, I woke up with a start, as if something had happened, as if something had dragged me out of slumber. I saw through the window that we were at a port. How could we stop at a port when we had no cargo to transport?

I came out of my cabin and saw all my co-workers dressed up, their bags on their backs and shoulders, leaving the ship. We had reached Mumbai.

As they walked down the gangway, I marvelled at the situation. They were all working for hefty pay packages, lakhs and lakhs of rupees, till just a few days ago; but now they were all unemployed.

Nearly all of them left immediately after disembarking. But Mr Shafi turned around and looked at the ship for some time before he walked away.

I did not leave. Instead, I went up to the deck. Captain Datt was sitting in a chair beside the railing and smoking a cigarette, totally lost in himself. Had the abyss inside his head thrown its anchor deep into his subconscious?

He looked up at me and asked, 'You didn't leave?'

'No. How could I? You're still here.'

'There's no use staying on. This is not a matter of a few days. It'll take a long time for the situation to improve.'

'I know.'

'Then why don't you leave?'

I lowered my eyes. He too said nothing. He took a last drag on his cigarette and threw it into the Arabian Sea.

'You don't want to return to the land either?' he asked as he stood up to leave. 'Did my abhorrence of land rub off on you as well?'

'No, no,' I said. 'It's not like that.'

'I'm going to the toilet.' He touched me on the shoulder. 'You too freshen up and meet me in the dining hall.'

It was in my bathroom that I felt I heard the noise of propellers. I shook my head, trying to throw the noise out of my ears. It didn't help. I don't know how I was hearing the noise of propellers when our ship was anchored at a port. I felt lonely and nervous. I felt as if I had been thrown off something, in the middle of nowhere. While bathing, while changing my clothes, while combing my hair, the noise of propellers kept ringing in my ears. I shook my head again, forcefully this time, and the noise stopped. I had succeeded in throwing it out of my ears.

I went and sat with Captain Datt at a table in the dining hall. We were the only people on the ship. The cook in the kitchen was the only other employee left on the ship and he would stay on with us till a decision was made by the shipping company. Captain Datt and I had toast, butter, boiled eggs and tea for breakfast and kept sitting at the table for an hour or so after that. Neither of us said a word.

I knew there was nothing left except ennui. There were other ships too, anchored at the port; all their shipping companies were out of work too.

Initially, passing the time on a stationary ship was difficult, but then I got used to it. I realised that I had no desire to return to land. So, had I too, like Captain Alok Datt, started abhorring land? What reason did I have to feel that way? Captain Datt hated land because of the violence that had been unleashed on it. Why did I hate it?

CHAPTER 13

# Birds

Three months passed on the ship. We—Captain Alok Datt and I—did not talk as much as we used to before the ship docked. Along with the ship, we too had thrown our anchors. He spent his time either writing in his diary or reading from it. In the beginning, he would get up early in the morning, go up to the deck, settle himself in his chair, and throw grains or popcorn all around him. When the cook or I went to call him for breakfast, he'd be surrounded by so many birds that it was hard to locate him amidst their fluttering wings. By the time we reached the third month of our stay on the ship, he had stopped throwing grains and popcorn for the birds.

Initially, I think the birds used to get angry with me. For, whenever I walked close to the captain, they fluttered their wings violently and flew away en masse from the ship. The noise of their fluttering wings seemed to ask me, 'Who are you? What business do you have here? Why don't you let us peck at the grains in peace?' But as the days passed, they seemed to recognise me; they would just move out of my path as I went to call Captain Datt for breakfast.

Birds consider docked ships their home. They build nests in the nooks and crevices of decked ships. Several birds built their nests on Jaldoot too. It was easier for pigeons because they did not build nests; they just claimed an entire cabin for themselves. There were eggs being incubated in some cabins, while hatchlings peeped from others. There were nests in the corridor between the rows of cabins, in the engine room and the control room, in any place with a safe surface or corner. Every morning, the corridor between the cabins would come alive with the chirping of birds. Captain Datt, however, was so lost in himself that I wondered if he even heard the birds right outside his cabin.

I knew that Captain Datt wasn't going to snap out of his thoughts, whether they were related to the ship or his own private life. He had gone to the local office of the Grand Eastern Shipping Company in Mumbai. Mr Sheikh, the chairman of the company, told him clearly that the company had got buried in debt; it would never do business again.

According to Mr Sheikh, Chinese corporations were major clients of their company. Three years ago, the Chinese market was so prosperous that the shipping company found it difficult to provide them with ships. In order to take advantage of the market in China, the company ordered three huge ships from a manufacturer in Germany. The recession, however, threw a spanner in all their deals. The ships were ready at the factory in Germany, but there was no new trade to be done and the shipping company did not have adequate funds to pay for the ships and bring them to Mumbai. On top of that, if the ships were not taken from the factory within the stipulated time, the shipping company would have to pay the company in Germany a demurrage charge every month, and the charge could run up to several hundred millions of rupees per month. In order to arrange for money, the Grand Eastern Shipping Company had decided to sell their old ships. However, the recession was so bad that no one was willing to buy the old ships even at heavily discounted rates. There was only one way now in which the shipping company could procure money: send the old ships to the ship-breaking yard and sell them as scrap. The management of the Grand Eastern Shipping Company had decided to raise funds for the demurrage charge by selling off Jaldoot as scrap.

I didn't see anything wrong with the way they had chosen to arrange for the funds. Sometime in the future, when the situation improved, they would again be in a position to buy news ships and perhaps employ all of us. So I did not understand why Captain Alok Datt had to lose sleep over this, why he tired himself so, why he neglected the birds that had made it their habit to peck on the grains and popcorn he threw for them. The birds surrounded Captain Datt as he sat on the deck. Staring at him, they too perhaps wondered what had come over the man, how he had changed.

Captain Datt was completely unmindful of the birds. I could see a crushing pain in his gaze when he looked at Jaldoot. He went to the control room and the engine room and touched the parts there as if it wasn't a ship he was touching but a human—a human who had fallen sick and needed care and therapy. I wondered why he was doing it. After all, it was just a ship, a structure made of iron that would be scrapped in a few days' time. Three new ships would soon take Jaldoot's place and, hopefully, we would all be reinstated. Certainly, it wasn't the first time that a senior seaman like Captain Alok Datt was working on a ship that was to be scrapped. I couldn't understand his morbid attachment to Jaldoot.

And then one day, he told me.

'There are still five years left for Jaldoot to be decommissioned. It will be scrapped not because it is old or because of an accident, but because of the greed and shortsightedness of the corporate world.'

CHAPTER 14

# Alang

The Mumbai cityscape glimmered in its affluence and indifference on the night our ship set out for the ship-breaking yard in Alang on the Gulf of Khambat in Gujarat. The ship was going to be scrapped, so the national flag had been taken down from its mast and replaced with a black flag.

Our crew on this final journey was rather small. Apart from Captain Datt and me, there were on board two engineers, two sailors, and the cook. Our crew was small, but we were not alone. We were accompanied by all those birds who had made the mistake of considering our ship their home. Disillusioned, they flew out of the ship and began to hover above us as it started moving. They flew out, then returned to their nests, then flew out again, then returned again. They couldn't fathom how their home had started moving at night. How could we tell them that their home was being taken to be broken down? And even if we did, what would they do with their nests and hatchlings, and the eggs which were yet to hatch?

The next morning, I saw Captain Alok Datt sitting on the deck. He looked calm. Or perhaps he was feigning calmness, for there was nothing more that he or any of us could do for our ship. Captain Datt had already instructed us on how to dock the ship. It was easy to send a ship sailing for the first time because only a pair of sloping ramps made of iron were enough to push it down into the water. Docking a ship at a ship-breaking yard was a different kettle of fish. The generators of the ship usually did not have enough fuel to push it to the shore. A ship meant to be broken down was dependent only on a high tide and strong winds to push it to the yard. Captain Datt explained to me that it was practically impossible to pull a ship as huge as Jaldoot using only cranes, so it was necessary that we ourselves devised a way to dock it.

I watched him closely. I couldn't believe that his calmness was for real. There was something, I felt, still churning inside him. I could see him retiring into his world of shadows, a world from which it would perhaps be impossible to extricate him.

He left the deck rather absent-mindedly. His leaving made me feel as if destiny had brought me face to face with yet another baffling disappearance or abandonment. Captain Datt's going away seemed to me akin to the mahout's disappearance into the forest. Soon after the mahout's disappearance, I had witnessed the elephant being mauled by wild dogs. Quite soon, this ship—huge, just like an elephant—too would be dismantled, mauled by machines.

I returned to the engine room where one of the engineers eagerly offered me a cup of coffee from a thermos. I drank the coffee and we began working. I got so busy in the engine room that for the next three hours I didn't have the time to think about anything else, not even Captain Datt. Later on, I'd realise that the moment Captain Datt *abandoned* me on the deck was the last time I saw him.

The captain had instructed us to stop the ship about a hundred nautical miles from the breaking yard. The ship, the sky, the sea, were all calm as we carried out Captain Datt's instructions. The scene changed only around midnight when the tide began to rise. The tumultuous sea began rattling the empty, stationary ship. Taking our cue, we started propelling the ship towards the shore. At nearly half past one in the night, we found what we'd been waiting for: the highest tide which would give the required push to the ship to move it. The wave nearly tossed the ship over. There lay before our eyes the largest graveyard for ships in the world.

I came to the engine room where the noise of the generators was deafening. I told the engineers to drop everything, settle down and tighten their seatbelts. In some time, Jaldoot crashed into the shore with such force that its bow rose high up.

We unclasped our seatbelts and immediately turned off the generators. I stood beside the generators till they had turned completely silent. We were all soaked in sweat when we came out of the engine room. Our hair was matted with smoke and our skin darkened. Once we were out on the deck, we saw that the entire vessel had plunged into darkness. Turning off the generators meant that there was no more power supply available to the ship. Those generators would not be turned on again. That was when it struck me that this ship which had become an integral part of my life would no longer be around.

In a matter of hours, it would be broken into pieces and its parts sold off.

Perhaps the birds understood the situation too. As soon as the ship plunged into darkness, the corridors and the deck were filled with birds flying around madly, as if looking for something they had lost or were about to lose. The crew were already on the deck where they hung a rope ladder with nearly a hundred rungs for us to get off the ship. I tiptoed over broken eggs and squirming hatchlings on the ground of the corridor to reach the deck. I saw the ground staff of the ship-breaking yard pulling and tugging at the rope ladder to check its strength before signalling us to start climbing down.

That's when a sailor asked, 'Where is the captain?'

The crew put down their bags and signalled at the yard workers to wait. We decided to go looking for Captain Alok Datt.

We split up. An engineer and I returned to the engine room, picked up a flashlight, and went into the depths of the ship.

The crash had already dismantled the ship. The machinery in the lower half of the ship, all of it built of strong iron, was either distorted or mangled. It was hard to tell which staircase started at which point and where it ended. The doors of the cabins had all come off, giving the dark cabins filled with bird nests and other garbage, an eerie, intimidating look. Doors broken off their hinges lay awkwardly in the corridors. We had to jump over them to traverse the passages.

We were panting when we reached Captain Datt's cabin. I was already speculating on what I would get to see there in case the captain was up to anything untoward.

The door of Captain Datt's cabin too had fallen off its hinge and lay on its side on the ground before the doorway. I gave it a kick and it fell flat on the floor, clearing the path for us to enter the cabin. We entered and saw that all the books had fallen off the shelves. The bottles had crashed and broken into pieces. We moved carefully amidst the sharp shards and pieces of glass. Among the shards lay Captain Datt's diary. I picked it up when the engineer wasn't watching and tucked it into my clothes. It was torn and several of its pages had been removed. Perhaps the captain had himself ripped out the pages.

I stood in the middle of the cabin for a long time, not knowing where to go or what to do next. Again and again, something the captain had told me during our conversations returned to my mind: 'Destruction and its consequences are the legacy we have received from our ancestors and that's exactly what we are going to pass on to our progenies.'

The engineer was restless, eager to leave the dark, ghostly ship. As we left the cabin and walked along the dark passage, I heard a chirping. Quite faint, weak, but a chirping nonetheless. There was a live bird somewhere, perhaps stuck. The chirping came from beneath the staircase that Captain Datt and I took to climb to the deck. There was a bird there. Perhaps it had its nest there, which had now been destroyed. Perhaps it was a nestling whose mother had died. I wanted to flash my light on the bird, but I stopped. What would be the use? What could I do for it? If it was a healthy, adult bird, it would come out on its own. If it was sick or injured, did I have any way to nurse it back to good health? And if it was a mere nestling, would it survive?

I forced myself to ignore the chirping and began climbing the stairs to the deck. When so many nations were drowning in debt in this sudden recession, did a mere bird have the strength to draw anyone's attention with its cries?

The engineer and I returned to the deck and met the rest of the crew there.

'He isn't here,' a sailor said.

'Where could he go?' the other engineer asked. 'We didn't see him climb down the rope ladder.'

The cook went to the railing and shouted at the workers below, 'Where is the captain?'

The workers couldn't hear him clearly.

'Where is our captain? Is he down there?' the cook shouted again.

The workers shook their heads. No.

'They're saying the captain hasn't left the ship,' the cook informed us.

As if something sparked within me, I turned and entered the depths of the ship again.

'Where are you going now?' The engineer who had accompanied me asked. And then he began following me. Gradually, the rest of the crew joined in.

I groped my way in the dark to where the lifeboats were kept. In the glow of our flashlights, we saw that one lifeboat was missing. We looked at the remaining lifeboats in silence, then at each other.

'Do we need to report this?' one of the crew members asked.

'What? He left in a lifeboat?' another crew member asked.

'When?'

'In that high tide? Was he all right?'

'Why?'

'Where?'

Our return to the deck was abuzz with speculation and conversations that led nowhere. I was quiet. I left unanswered all the questions I was asked.

I put Captain Alok Datt's diary—or whatever remained of it—in my backpack. With my backpack on my shoulders, I walked towards the rope ladder. I looked at the other ships beached there, each one awaiting its death like a solitary elephant that had come away from its herd just to die.

When I placed my foot on the first rung of the rope ladder, I thought of going back to look for Captain Alok Datt again. Had he really left on a lifeboat? Where was he now?

But hadn't the captain himself left us? Had he wanted to stay with us, he would have. He would have waited with us for the high tide, he would have experienced the crash with a seatbelt fastened around his body, he would have seen us switching off the generators, he would have shown us the rope ladder, he would have harried us to clear the ship as soon as possible. But he hadn't. He had just walked away. He instructed us on how to dock the ship at the breaking yard and just walked away. Disappeared, in fact. Perhaps he wished to live away from the world that we were all destined to return to.

Who knew where Captain Datt was? I didn't. Like I didn't know where the mahout went that night, leaving me on the back of the elephant. Like I didn't know where my sister went when I got sudden news from the village that she had left with the Dada Log from the forest.

The staff of the ship-breaking yard began climbing up the ship using the rope ladder as soon as our feet touched the shore. Everyone on the crew left, one by one. But I did not leave immediately. I watched as they began breaking down Jaldoot.

I knew I was like an animal, unmoved by events. The emotion I had felt when all the lights on the ship went out after the generators were turned off had left me. I was looking at the ship being broken down not because I felt anything for it but because I wanted to see how a ship could be broken down.

I thought that the ship let out a cry of agony as the cranes pulled its parts apart. I thought that the cables and angles and beams and everything in the innards of the ship, which were now exposed, resembled the entrails of the elephant after it had been disembowelled alive by the wild dogs. I felt as if the ship was staring at me with its dying eyes like an elephant had once done in its death throes. But I did not let any surge of emotion drown me. I just looked on.

CHAPTER 15

# Returning

From Alang, I went to Bhavnagar. At the railway station in Bhavnagar, I waited for four hours for my train to arrive; and it was only an hour before its arrival that I realised how dirty my face and clothes were. There was soot all over me, the soot from the generators. I washed my face with water and soap and then I was ready to board the train.

I journeyed for two days. From Bhavnagar to Ahmedabad and from Ahmedabad to Raipur. I wanted to erase all the memories of the world I was leaving behind. I wanted to return to where I came from, where I actually belonged. I wanted to return to silence, to Silence.

Settled on my berth, I reflected on what I had gained—or lost—in my journey so far. What had I returned with? What had I found?

Nothing, except a diary, tattered and discarded. Abandoned.

Upon reading the pages of Captain Alok Datt's diary, I could tell that he found it difficult to accept himself as human. He had started seeing his soul as a skeleton—hollow and useless. Not a word in his diary indicated any sort of lust for life, any glory in being born as a human being. There was a sorrowful account of the world and its destruction on every page of his diary. He had mentioned the various kinds of violence inflicted upon human societies—which he had already told me about—in his diary.

*'Modern industrial enterprises are a type of carnage. Industrial cartels subject others to death for profits, and these destructive endeavours are persevering . Governments contribute to this carnage. And this carnage is invisible despite having long-standing effects.'*

No wonder Captain Datt did not wish to return to this world.

The train hurtled over shiny tracks, leaving everything behind. I hurtled ahead on that train, leaving the life on the ocean behind. I sat with the tattered diary in my hands the entire night. I don't remember when I fell asleep and how many stations passed in the meantime.

A golden dawn illuminated the compartment when I woke up. The train had slowed down—perhaps that was what woke me up, the slowing down of the train, an interruption in the otherwise constant movement.

It stopped in the middle of an open field. I got up from my berth and went and washed my face at the wash basin. Wiping my face with a handkerchief, I peered out of the door of the compartment. The morning breeze was refreshing. I got down from the train and walked into the field. There were cows grazing on tall, wild grass. I ran my fingers through the grass. A cow stopped grazing and looked up at me. A memory came fluttering into my mind, of the cow who only allowed my sister to milk her. I walked to the cow and stroked her head and jowls. She inched closer to me and rubbed her body against mine.

The train hooted. I went and boarded my compartment. I had the desire to add some of the beauty and tranquility of the field to the pages of Captain Datt's diary, but what did I know of writing? My hand, quite involuntarily, went into my trouser's pocket. I grabbed the stone named Passion and turned it between my fingers. I decided to leave the diary as it was. I knew I wouldn't be able to adequately balance the ugliness described in Captain Datt's diary with the limited vocabulary I had.

CHAPTER 16

# Time

It wasn't easy for me to enter the forest this time. Under no circumstances could I take the route that I had taken before, the route that had been carved out for an alleged development of Bastar. I had to take the secret routes along which I had come out of the forest. I had to take the pathways hidden behind the bushes. I had to take the tracks concealed by rocks. I had to walk on those tracks to look for Silence, who was trying to bring order to a place devastated at the hands of the Salwa Judum and the Naga Batallion. I couldn't spot signs of any major incident, but I could tell that the rebels had gained the upper hand.

As I walked ahead, I had the feeling that the forest had united itself following the devastation. It had regained its rhythm. I heard the strains of trumpets and the beating of drums. They contained in them not only the songs of the ancestors but also some secret messages. Upon walking further, I saw the people who had been left behind in the villages standing in united, close-knit groups. I found the relief camps empty and abandoned and wondered where everybody had gone. Close to fifty thousand people could not just disappear all of a sudden.

Perhaps those fifty thousand internally displaced people had ended up at a crossroads where one path went out of the forest and the villages towards the big cities where there were opportunities for livelihood, while the other path went into the forest where the rebels fighting for their rights and land had positioned themselves with weapons in their hands. How many of those fifty thousand people had migrated to Andhra Pradesh in search of two square meals and how many had stayed on in the forests to fight for what had been snatched away from them—this could perhaps be fodder for sociologists.

I had no use for any such analysis. I was only to pass through all that had been destroyed, past the statues of martyrs and past the graves marked with sickle-and-hammer figurines. And none of these were conclusive. They were just symbols that two opposing factions had erected. Pages after pages would be written about the warring parties, but of what use would they be? Who would write about the people who had been ruined while they were still alive? Who would write about those adolescent single mothers who bore the illegitimate scions of men from the paramilitary forces? Who would write about the weak and ailing elderly people who had lost their homes and were forced to stay on in abandoned relief camps? I saw no hope in their eyes as they stared at me with empty eyes; just the way there was no hope in the eyes of an elephant being disembowelled alive, or the way a functioning ship had stared at me while being dismantled.

I reached the same spot outside my village where I had, not very long ago, picked up two stones. One had dropped somewhere on the ground; the other had found its way into my pocket and my life. I had no use anymore for the stone that was in my pocket. I took it and flung it far away, in the direction of what used to be my village. Then I took the path towards the forest, where I had once followed an elephant and then, Silence.

There were no more check posts nor policemen on that path. There was only the sound of dried leaves crumbling beneath my feet. I reached the banyan tree under which I had witnessed two instances of violence—one that had grown out of hunger, the other out of retribution.

The shade of that banyan tree had taken on a new look. It wasn't secret or solitary anymore. It was abuzz with activity. The space had been cleared and turned into a camp for the rebels. There were several tents there, and cadres, wearing their guerrilla fatigues, and they were engaged in their daily tasks. Some of them were washing clothes, others were cooking or boiling water for drinking, while the rest were teaching a group of children. I walked close to a clothesline where several shirts and trousers had been hung out to dry. I sensed something as I reached that clothesline. I sensed Silence.

I moved a washed piece of clothing aside and peered. I saw her. She was sitting on a mat. She had a needle and thread in her hands, a shirt in her lap, and a few uniforms around her. A pair of crutches lay beside her. I looked at the crutches, then at her left leg. It was amputated below the knee. I kept looking at her amputated leg for some time. Then I looked at her face.

Her hair had greyed, but she looked as capable and determined as ever.

I didn't call out to her. Her companions noticed me and let me be. Perhaps they would go and inform her. But for the time being, they left both of us alone—she, to her sewing; I, to watching her sew.

The things that Time makes us do! One day, Time makes a boy pick up a stone and leads him out of a forest to the wide, open ocean; another day, it makes a girl discard her basket of forest fruits and take up guns. One day, Time takes a girl away from her brother; another day, it makes that brother come looking for his sister—the sister he had named Silence.

# Author's Acknowledgements

I am grateful to

Ernesto Cardenal
Gautam Navlakha
Sudha Bharadwaj
Manzoor Ahtesham
Rajkumar Soni
and
Nanu,

who contributed, in their own way, to the creation of this novel.

# Translator's Acknowledgements

In translating *Kaale Adhyaay* into *I Named My Sister Silence,* I benefitted immensely from the support, guidance and encouragement of the following people and organisations:

Aditi Maheshwari Goyal and Vani Prakashan

Anees Salim

Annie Zaidi

Jayapriya Vasudevan and Jacaranda Literary Agency

Madhuri Vijay

Minakshi Thakur and Westland Books

Pratik Infotech, Ghatsila

Priyanka Sandilya

Rozy Gawde

and, above all,

Manoj Rupda.

An excerpt from *I Named My Sister Silence* was published in *Hammock Mag.*

All errors and omissions are mine, and I take full responsibility for the same.